"You're not seducing me!"

"Why? Because I ignored you this afternoon? Honey, what's going on between you and me has nothing to do with getting along, or making a commitment or even exchanging phone numbers. And right now your body's telling me you feel the same things I do."

"You are so crude!"

"I'm certainly not hearts and flowers." There. It was out. The thing Cooper had wanted to deny all day. The thing he wanted Zoe to understand. The thing he needed for both of them to get beyond.

"I'm a hearts-and-flowers kind of girl."

"Hey, I didn't say I wouldn't be romantic."

"I don't want romance. I want love."

Dear Reader,

As the days get shorter and the approaching holidays bring a buzz to the crisp air, nothing quite equals the joy of reuniting with family and catching up on the year's events. This month's selections all deal with family matters, be it making one's own family, dealing with family members or doing one's family duty.

Desperate to save his family ranch, the hero in Elizabeth Harbison's *Taming of the Two* (#1790) enters into a bargain that could turn a pretend relationship into the real deal. This is the second title in the SHAKESPEARE IN LOVE trilogy. A die-hard bachelor gets a taste of what being a family man is like when he rescues a beautiful stranger and her adorable infant from a deadly blizzard, in Susan Meier's *Snowbound Baby* (#1791)—part of the author's BRYANT BABY BONANZA continuity. Carol Grace continues her FAIRY TALE BRIDES miniseries with *His Sleeping Beauty* (#1792) in which a woman sheltered by her overprotective parents gains the confidence to strike out on her own after her handsome—but cynical—neighbor catches her sleepwalking in his garden! Finally, in *The Marine and Me* (#1793), the next installment in Cathie Linz's MEN OF HONOR series, a soldier determined to outwit his matchmaking grandmother and avoid the marriage landmine gets bushwhacked by his supposedly dowdy neighbor.

Be sure to come back next month when Karen Rose Smith and Shirley Jump put their own spins on Shakespeare and the Dating Game, respectively!

Happy reading.

Ann Leslie Tuttle
Associate Senior Editor

Please address questions and book requests to:
Silhouette Reader Service
U.S.: 3010 Walden Ave., P.O. Box 1325, Buffalo, NY 14269
Canadian: P.O. Box 609, Fort Erie, Ont. L2A 5X3

SUSAN MEIER

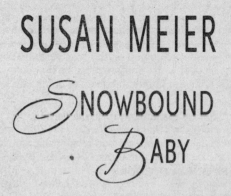

SNOWBOUND BABY

Bryant Baby
Bonanza

SILHOUETTE *Romance*®
Published by Silhouette Books
America's Publisher of Contemporary Romance

SILHOUETTE BOOKS

ISBN 0-373-19791-8

SNOWBOUND BABY

Copyright © 2005 by Susan Meier

SUSAN MEIER

is one of eleven children, and though she's yet to write a book about a big family, many of her books explore the dynamics of "unusual" family situations, such as large work "families," bosses who behave like overprotective fathers, or "sister" bonds created between friends. Because she has more than twenty nieces and nephews, children also are always popping up in her stories. Many of the funny scenes in her books are based on experiences raising her own children or interacting with her nieces and nephews.

She was born and raised in western Pennsylvania and continues to live in Pennsylvania.

Snowbound Holiday Punch

2 tsp whole cloves
1 tsp allspice
4 sticks cinnamon
$1/2$ c sugar
$2^1/_2$ c water
1 c frozen lemonade
1 c frozen orange juice
2 pint cranberry juice
$1^1/_2$ quarts ice water

Combine spices, sugar and $2^1/_2$ cups water in saucepan. Simmer ten minutes, strain and cool. Combine lemonade, orange juice and cranberry juice and add to spice mixture. Just before serving, add ice water. Pour over ice in punch bowl for serving.

Ginger ale can be substituted for ice water.

Chapter One

"Son of a..."

Cooper Bryant cut off his curse, needing all of his mental and physical energy to maneuver his eighteen-wheeler around a Toyota that was stuck in the middle of the snow-covered mountain road. Passing the car, he peered down, ready to make a gesture to let the driver know exactly how he felt about people who blocked the way. But he saw the stranded motorist was a young woman. And she had a baby in the back seat.

Shoot!

Well, he couldn't stop to help. Ironically, the short-cut that he'd cajoled from the turnpike tollbooth attendant hadn't allowed him to outrun the storm, but had, instead, slowed him down. The twisting, winding route up the Western Pennsylvania mountain couldn't be taken with any kind of speed. The curves all seemed to hug the edge of the world. And once a semi lost speed climbing a steep slope, it was impossible to get it back. If Cooper stopped now, his truck would stay exactly where it was until the state plowed away the snow.

He made it another couple hundred feet, but his wheels began hesitating. Cooper knew his truck wasn't going to reach the top. Unlike the driver in the Toyota who had simply parked where her car had stopped, he eased his vehicle onto the first shoulder he found that had more than six inches of space between his truck and a cliff, and cut the engine.

He didn't like wasting precious hours like this—however, lost time was better than a wreck. He didn't have one of the elaborate, expensive trucks with sleeping quarters, but he'd passed several hunting cabins. One of them, if not all of them, probably had a woodstove. He had two sandwiches, a thermos of coffee, soap, towels, a blanket and a shaving kit. He could be comfortable for the night, and rested when he got back on the road tomorrow.

Hoisting his backpack of supplies, Cooper jumped out of the cab and into the crystallized white snow. He had switched his trademark cowboy boots for thick work boots at the truck stop off the turnpike exit, but he still had his black Stetson and denim jacket. Unfortunately, they weren't much against the bite of the unforgiving mountain wind. Cooper was an Arkansas boy, born and bred, but he'd transplanted himself to Texas where he and a buddy had bought a ranch. For the past three years he'd been saving the money he made driving truck to increase the herd and he'd been everywhere from Oregon to Florida. He'd experienced cold, wind, even snow…but not like this.

He tucked himself more tightly inside his jacket as

he made his way down the hill. Only about twenty feet from his truck he saw a cabin. Small, with chipping white paint and a sagging roof, the structure was nonetheless good enough for the night. He was about to turn down the snow-covered lane when he remembered the young woman in the Toyota.

And her baby.

Shoot!

He sighed. He wasn't much on company. Ever. His beliefs were so far out of sync with those of the general population that every time he opened his mouth he seemed to get into an argument. In his reckless youth, that had led to some nasty bar fights. Even his own brothers had said he was always making trouble and kicked him out of their lives eight years ago.

Determined to keep his world peaceful, he wasn't somebody who went looking for human contact. So, fate should have known better than to throw a stranded woman in his path. He might be able to help her find shelter, but he wasn't about to play gin rummy until the snowplow came through. If she was a chatterbox who needed constant entertainment, she'd get on his nerves and he'd probably end up making her cry.

Yeah, this was going to be peachy.

Still, he started walking to her car. He didn't get too far before he realized it was at least two football fields away. If he went down the mountain to offer the woman the opportunity to share a cabin, he wouldn't simply be going the length of two football fields to get her. He would have to walk those two football fields back up again.

Shoot.

He didn't want to let a mama and baby freeze to

death, but she should have known better than to travel on a day like this.

Cooper continued down the mountain anyway. Slipping and sliding as the powerful wind pushed him along the steep slope, he traveled the distance in what he knew had to be record time. In only a few minutes, he rounded a curve and saw the Toyota. It was now covered with snow, and he could see no sign of exhaust coming out the back. Cooper guessed the driver was either gone or she'd quit running her motor to save gas for the long night. Though he knew having her along would be nothing but irritation to his already frayed nerves, he couldn't stop a surge of male ego. If she was still in that car, she would be really glad to see him.

With the wind urging him on, he half ran the rest of the way, almost losing his balance twice on the icy incline. When he reached the car, he tapped on the driver's side window. The snow-covered glass began a very slow descent, but it stopped after about four inches. Then the barrel of a gun greeted him.

Cooper jumped back. *What the hell!*

"Get lost," the young woman yelled. "I don't have any money and I'm not willing to share my car with you. I have a baby."

"I don't want to share your car. My truck's parked just up the road." Cooper paused long enough to curse under his breath because his heart was jumping like a jackrabbit. Only an idiot used a gun so carelessly. "Look, I passed three hunting cabins on my walk down the hill. I saw you on my way up but couldn't stop. If you want, you can spend the night in a cabin with me, and I'll take care of the woodstove. If you don't, that's cool, too."

He waited for a response but got none. Fool woman! Just like a mare he'd bought two years ago. Didn't have a whit of common sense.

He gave her another thirty seconds. Still nothing.

"Suit yourself," he called, then turned and began re-climbing the hill, the howling wind nearly blowing him down again. He knew it couldn't be any warmer than ten degrees. When the sun set even that scant heat would disappear. With the wind chill it would be so far below zero the number would be irrelevant. Anyone without proper shelter would freeze to death. Even if that kid had a blanket—*four* blankets—she and her baby would freeze to death.

Shoot!

He let the wind blow him back down to her car, then tapped on the window and jumped out of the way as the glass lowered, just in case she aimed the barrel of the gun at him again.

"It's going to be below zero tonight. You are not going to survive in that car."

"We'll be fine."

"No, you won't!" Getting angry now, he tried her door but it was locked. "If you didn't have a baby, I wouldn't give a flying fig about you freezing to death. But you've got a kid. You have to be reasonable."

"I am reasonable." She sighed and rolled down the window. Cooper couldn't help noticing her blond hair, clear pink skin and cornflower blue eyes. "Look, I called a friend. Any minute now I'll be rescued."

At that Cooper laughed. "Rescued? Haven't you heard the weather?"

Her pretty eyes narrowed. "Yes and no. I heard about

a snowstorm, but it's always snowing here. I live on the other side of this mountain. I'm so used to the snow I hardly pay attention."

"Well, you should have paid attention because this is a blizzard." He drew in a quick breath and his lungs rebelled at the cold. "The temperatures are falling faster than normal. They're predicting two feet of snow. If your friend is smart, he'll stay home."

Waiting for her reply, he blew on his hands. Even with gloves his fingers were going numb.

When she said nothing, his patience suddenly evaporated and he yelled, "Come out in thirty seconds or I'll break your car window to save your kid."

He swore he heard her sigh with disgust, but decided it had to be the wind. Then she kicked open her door and pushed herself out. A blast of air caught her pale hair and fanned it away from her head.

More concerned with getting them safely to shelter, he barely noticed the pretty feathery locks. "Where's your hat?"

She turned and her blue eyes pinned him with an exasperated look. "It's in the car."

"Good, put it on and let's get the hell going. It's cold."

She said, "Right," then bent and reached inside her vehicle. Her red leather jacket only came to her waist and when she stretched he got a full view of the enticing curve of her bottom.

Cooper quickly turned away. Since she had a baby, the woman was obviously married, and staring at her behind, no matter how nicely rounded, was inappropriate.

The wind kicked up. From the back of her car, the woman pulled out a white plastic contraption lined with pink and navy blue plaid padding. She set it on the driver's seat, then reached into the back again and extracted a baby wearing a pink snowsuit and wrapped in a pink blanket. She sat the kid in the padding of the white plastic thing. When she looped a handle from beneath and snapped it into place, Cooper guessed the contraption was some kind of baby carrier.

"I should take her," Cooper said, assuming the baby was a girl because of all the pink.

"I'll carry her," the woman disagreed, leaving the baby on the front seat of her car so she could dig out an enormous diaper bag. Pink plaid to match the travel seat, it was stuffed to capacity and looked more like a trash can with a strap. "You take this."

She shoved the two-ton diaper bag into Cooper's arms just as a gust of wind hit him and he nearly fell backward. But he didn't. He didn't fall. He didn't curse. He didn't even yelp. Instead he saw the nice, quiet evening he could have had blow away on a frigid blast of air.

He nodded up the hill. "The cabins are this way."

He turned to begin the upward trek, but she caught his arm with her glove-covered fingers.

Everything inside of Cooper stilled. It had been so long since anybody had dared to touch him—except in a fight—that his hands automatically curled into fists. But before he instinctively took a punch, he looked into her round blue eyes and a tingling sensation exploded in his gut. Now he understood why she mistrusted him. She was gorgeous and he was about to spend the night with her.

With her body shielding the open car door and Daphne from the wind, Zoe Montgomery stared at the man in front of her, pretending her shivers were from cold, not from fear. She shouldn't have touched him. Until she'd touched him he'd seemed like a grumpy Kola bear. Now he looked like an angry panther. His green eyes glittered, his hands were fisted and his body was stiff, poised and ready to strike.

Tall and lean, with a black Stetson pulled low over his eyes, her rescuer was definitely all male, but he also had an air of trouble. For all she knew he could be an escaped convict. Well, actually, he'd said he drove a truck and she'd seen an eighteen-wheeler pass her about ten minutes after her car had simply stopped. But truckers weren't always reputable. Some were hellions who took advantage of roaming the country doing all kinds of crazy things and this guy obviously had a hair trigger.

Still, not all truckers were bad. Some were Good Samaritans. Touchy though he was, this man could be one of those who saw it as his responsibility to help anyone on the road when problems hit.

Also, her options were limited. Whoever he was, he was right. If her car hadn't died because it was old, but because it couldn't handle the snow on the mountain, then LuAnn—her rescuer—wasn't getting up here, either. And if the temperature was about to plummet, Zoe knew she and Daphne would freeze to death in the car.

She wasn't sure she was any safer in a cabin with a stranger, but technically she didn't have to "stay" with him. There were lots of hunting cabins on this mountain. Many of them were in clusters. He could sleep in one. She and Daphne could sleep in another.

She took a silent, life-sustaining breath. Not only was that a safe plan, but also it was a smart plan. He didn't look like the kind of guy who wanted anyone invading his space, and she didn't need anyone helping her. When her ex-husband had discovered Zoe was pregnant and left her, she'd gotten a crash course in taking care of herself. Brad had moved on so quickly, he hadn't bothered divorcing her. She'd had to divorce him. And even though there was a court order filed for child support, Brad didn't honor it.

Zoe knew some men saw responsibility as a frightening trap, but more than that, she'd learned the value of standing on her own two feet and she wasn't letting anybody steal her independence away from her. She liked taking care of herself. This trucker didn't want her around and she didn't want him around. Separate cabins worked.

She pulled her fingers off his forearm and smiled slightly to take the sting out of her forwardness of touching him. "Or we could go down the mountain *with* the wind rather than against it. I live around here, remember? This part of the mountain is used almost exclusively for hunting. We're bound to find more cabins on the way down. In fact, we'll probably find clusters of cabins," she added, preparing him for the fact that they would stay in different shelters, if he hadn't already decided that himself.

He grunted as he hoisted the diaper bag on his shoulder where it settled beside his backpack. Then he turned and began walking down the hill.

Zoe grabbed Daphne's baby carrier from the front seat of the car, slammed the door, and followed him. The wind picked up. Swirling along the ground, it gathered fallen snow and propelled icy crystals upward, causing them to slap against Zoe's face. She pulled Daphne's blanket loosely over her head to shield her from the blasts, then lifted the carrier to chest height and slanted it toward her to provide even more protection for her baby.

"By the way, I'm Zoe Montgomery," she shouted to be heard above the wind. "And this is my daughter, Daphne."

For several seconds the trucker said nothing and Zoe worried that he wouldn't tell her his name. Not that she really *needed* to know his name, but if he wouldn't tell it, there could be a reason. Which took her back to her concern that he might be a criminal. Or worse, he could be a sex offender who had unspeakable plans for her. His not telling her his name was not a good sign.

Adrenaline pumped into her bloodstream and she remembered the gun in her jacket pocket. As a single mother, who lived alone on the edge of a small town that was too close to the turnpike, she frequently carried. Her cousins had shown her everything she needed to know about guns when they'd taught her to hunt, so she wasn't an amateur. And she also wasn't a hothead. She wouldn't arbitrarily shoot this trucker, but if he tried anything she wouldn't hesitate to defend herself and her daughter.

But right now, because they weren't too far from her car, simply running back to her vehicle and locking herself in was much smarter than shooting somebody.

She was formulating her plan of how to most effectively bolt when he said, "I'm Cooper Bryant."

So grateful she nearly collapsed with relief, Zoe said, "Well, it's nice to meet you, Cooper Bryant."

But Cooper Bryant said nothing. Either he didn't agree that it was nice to meet her or he wasn't the kind of guy to make small talk. Fine. She'd already figured out he was a loner. She respected that. He would probably jump for joy when she told him she preferred her own cabin and was perfectly capable of keeping a fire going all night.

They struggled another ten feet down the mountain. With every step they took, the temperature seemed to fall. The inside of Zoe's nose began to freeze. She huddled the baby carrier closer to her chest, protecting Daphne. She didn't need a thermometer to know it was much colder than it was even ten minutes ago. This storm was worse than any she'd ever seen.

The stranger beside her tapped her arm. Rather than try to speak above the wind that now roared through the trees and hollows, he pointed to the left. Cuddling Daphne's carrier against her, Zoe squinted, trying to make out what he apparently saw, but the only things in her line of vision were the black trunks of barren trees and swirling white snow. Visibility was down to about three feet. And that was another problem. If the wind and snow took away their ability to see, they could easily get lost in the woods.

She shook her head, indicating she saw nothing, and he caught her arm and hauled her across the road and up the slope into the woods.

Clinging to the baby carrier, which bounced precariously because of the trucker's hold on her arm, Zoe barely kept up with him. Fear churned through her at the way he was dragging her as if she were a kidnap victim. In her head she said every prayer she knew, hoping she hadn't gotten herself and her baby into terrible trouble, as the stranger propelled her through the woods, almost toppling her when he turned her to walk into the oncoming wind again. She gasped for breath, and righted herself, tightening her hold on Daphne. But as she did, she suddenly saw what he must have seen—what had motivated him to shove her through the forest.

A *house!*

Even if they had to spend the night, they would have a bathroom, food…and be among people! She wouldn't be alone with him!

Trying to run in the deep snow while hugging a bulky baby carrier, Zoe nearly fell twice. But her escort was running, too. She'd never felt the temperature fall so quickly and knew they had to get to shelter *now* or die.

With her boots clumped with snow, she stumbled on the front porch steps. When Cooper Bryant reached the top, he turned and grabbed the baby carrier from her hands, hauling it to his side before he caught Zoe's hand and pulled her up, too.

Still holding Daphne's seat, he ran across the plank porch to the door and pounded. Huddling into her insubstantial leather jacket and shivering violently, Zoe noticed there were no lights on in the house. A new fear tumbled through her. If there was no one home, they were in big trouble. God only knew how far they would have to go to the next shelter. And even if they did easily find another building, there was no guarantee it would have a stove. And if they found a cabin with a stove, there was no guarantee it would have wood.

If this house didn't pan out, there was a very good possibility she and Daphne would die.

"Here!"

Cooper Bryant shoved Daphne's baby carrier at Zoe and she caught it in trembling hands, again clutching Daphne close to her to protect her from the freezing wind. Cooper Bryant reached into his back pocket and retrieved his wallet. Just as quickly, he pulled out a credit card. Before Zoe realized what he was doing, he was sliding the card into the space between the doorknob and wood frame.

"You can't!"

He peered at her from beneath his Stetson. His green eyes glittered with annoyance. The angles and planes of his face were drawn in stern lines. Yelling to be heard above the roar of the wind through the trees, he said, "In case you haven't noticed, we don't have a choice."

He shimmied the card a few times, jiggling the doorknob as he did. The wind howled. Frigid air pricked at Zoe's cheeks. The lock on the door gave and Cooper shoved against the wood closure, opening it.

He grabbed Daphne's seat and Zoe's arm, propelling both Zoe and her baby into the house before him. Still holding Daphne, he slammed the door closed and for ten seconds or so they stood in the entryway of the simple two-story frame house, just breathing.

When it sunk in that they were out of the cold and safe, Zoe reached for Daphne, taking the handle of her baby carrier from Cooper Bryant's hand. They might be out of danger from the elements, but the ease with which this man had gotten them into a locked house increased her fears about him. Worse, she couldn't send him out into the cold to look for another shelter. Visibility was so bad now that he might not get back to the road.

"You're very good with a lock."

He returned the credit card to his wallet. "I knew this probably wouldn't be much of a lock."

She swallowed. "Really?"

He sighed. "I'm not a criminal. It's just that this house is so far out in the woods I'm surprised the owner bothers with locks at all. I'm from a very small town in Arkansas where locks are more or less for show, so people frequently forget their keys. Everybody in Porter's good with a credit card."

Cooper reached for the light switch. At his touch, the entryway lit. "Hey, we're in luck. If the electricity is on, that means there's likely a furnace and maybe even food in the fridge." He walked down the corridor and flipped a second switch, turning on another light and revealing the square corner of a bed in the room at the end of the hall.

"And here's a thermostat. It's set at fifty-five—just enough to keep the pipes from freezing. The person who owns this place obviously planned to be away awhile." He shifted the knob of the gadget to the left and the sound of a furnace rumbling to life came up from the basement.

Zoe glanced around nervously. "I don't feel right about this."

"You'd rather freeze to death?"

"No. But this is somebody's *home.*"

Cooper tossed Daphne's diaper bag to the floor along with his backpack before he removed his jacket, revealing a red plaid work shirt and nice-fitting jeans.

Zoe blinked. She'd already noticed that he was handsome, but in the silence of the foyer she was suddenly taking note of other things. For one, he was older. He had the air of experience that made a man sexy. Add that to his dark, dangerous, mysterious personality and he was one seductive guy.

She swallowed. Luckily, that was exactly the opposite of the kind of man she wanted. She was no longer "into" sexy guys.

Once he'd hooked his coat on a peg, he glanced around. "I don't think this is somebody's home. From the setting on the furnace and the dust on that TV," he said, pointing into a sitting room off to their left, "it looks more like a weekend retreat."

"It still belongs to somebody."

"Who would probably welcome us to spend the night in his house rather than freeze to death." He grabbed his backpack and slung it over his shoulder, then like a boss accustomed to giving orders, or a chauvinist who thought all women were pea-brains, he nudged Zoe to look down the hall. "There's your bedroom. You can have the one on the first floor to be closer to the kitchen since you have a kid. I'm going upstairs."

She tried to pretend she didn't notice his high-handedness and smiled graciously. "Don't you want to wait until I fix us something to eat?"

He patted the backpack. "I have a thermos of coffee and two sandwiches. No need for us to even speak another word."

Though Zoe had planned for them to separate, something about his tone confused her. She hadn't asked for his help. He had volunteered it, yet he was acting as if she was an unwanted thorn in his side. "You're leaving?"

"Think of it as me giving you your privacy. I don't need to entertain you just because I rescued you."

There was that tone again, the one that said having her around was a huge inconvenience. She couldn't argue that he hadn't rescued her. Not realizing the severity of the storm, she would have waited for LuAnn until it was too dark to find shelter. So, technically, he had rescued her. But she'd certainly never asked him to entertain her.

"No one said you had to. In fact, I was going to suggest you find a different cabin once we were settled."

"Right," Cooper scoffed, starting up the steps.

Zoe knew she should have let him go, but she hated that she'd never gotten the chance to prove to her ex-husband that she wasn't a wimp, that she wouldn't have smothered him, that he could have stayed with her if he'd just given her a chance. She wasn't letting another man on the face of this earth believe she was a clingy female. She was defending herself. "I did intend to take care of myself."

Cooper stopped walking and sighed. "Oh, come on. A woman who looks like you doesn't ever have to worry about taking care of herself."

Zoe felt her eyes widen at the insult. "I'm a single mother. I have to know how to handle anything that comes along."

"And that's why you called somebody—a man, no doubt—and were waiting in your car."

"LuAnn would be insulted to hear you call her a man." Zoe drew a quick, bolstering breath. "I didn't realize the storm was as bad as it was or I would have looked for shelter, not called someone to come and get me."

He shook his head, and didn't even try to hide his smirk. "Right."

She gaped at him. "What kind of experience do you have with women anyway?"

"Enough to know that the really good-looking ones take advantage of their assets."

This time her mouth fell open. "As if good-looking men are any better! I married a good-looking man and he left me alone to have his baby. While I was fighting morning sickness and wondering how I'd pay the bills, he used *his assets* to very quickly replace me, as if to prove to me he didn't need me. So don't stand there like the pot calling the kettle black."

Clearly exasperated with her, he said, "Look, I'm—"

Zoe didn't want to hear what he had to say. The best way to prove she could handle any problem that came along would simply be to do it. To hell with him and his opinion. "Save your piddly explanation for someone who cares. You and your thermos of coffee can go up-stairs. I want a good man, not just a good-looking man. You and *your assets* aren't needed down here."

Chapter Two

At the top of the steps Cooper found two bedrooms. He peered into the first, which had two single beds, then looked into the second and found a queen-sized bed with a thick comforter.

If the huge bed hadn't won him over, the thought of being wrapped in a comforter would have. His toes had long ago frozen. He didn't think the inside of his nose would ever be the same and he was sure his Arkansas-transplanted-to-Texas bones now had ice chips for marrow.

He tossed his backpack on the dusty dresser and sat on the bed to pull off his work boots and rub his feet. Though he had ratcheted up the furnace, the house wouldn't be warm for a while, if it truly heated up at all in the face of the biting wind. He massaged his sock-covered feet, trying to increase circulation, but in the quiet of the bedroom, he could hear Zoe Montgomery's movements below him.

Guilt tapped him on the shoulder, but he ignored it. He hadn't come upstairs because he liked to be alone. That was just a perk. He'd left to show her she was perfectly safe with him. She was a pretty girl with a face and figure that could set any man to drooling, and her physical appearance probably caused most men to make at least one pass at her. That was the best explanation for why she was skeptical of help from a man. Undoubtedly lots of the men who had offered her assistance in the past had counted upon something in return—most likely sex.

But Cooper wasn't interested. Well, he *was* interested if she was looking for a quick roll in the hay. But he was just about positive she wasn't. She'd admitted in her parting shot that her marriage had failed, so she was available. But she'd also said she wanted a good man, not merely a good-looking man, and when a woman said that it usually meant she was seeking a commitment. Rolls in the hay were not commitment-based. The way Cooper had it figured, she was one of those women who was searching for that special man who could make her trust again.

And Cooper was not anybody's special man so it was best to nip that fairy tale in the bud. God only knew how long they would be stranded together. Having felt the sting of the cold and seen the rapid rate of the snowfall, he was beginning to understand the biggest difference between a "storm" and a "blizzard" was that storms were a nuisance and blizzards were deadly. Smart people stayed indoors for the duration of a blizzard.

On top of that, as a trucker, Cooper had enough experience with highways and departments of transportation to realize that rarely traveled, two-lane roads used for shortcuts weren't the first to be cleared. He and Zoe were stuck in this house for the next twenty-four hours—at least. His actual guess was that they were here for the weekend. He didn't anticipate getting back to his truck before Monday morning.

But as long as he and Zoe had minimal contact, that might not be a problem. It was December twelfth. Though his brothers had bought the mortgage to his ranch and given him until Christmas to pay it off, he still had thirteen days. It would take him three to deliver his load and only another two to drive his certified check to Arkansas and put it in the hands of his brothers' lawyer. He had absolutely no intention of placing the check in Ty's hands, as he had been instructed in the letter advising him his brothers were calling in his debt. No court in the land would side with them if they tried to take his ranch just because he'd given the check to the lawyer, rather than directly to his brother.

Thirteen days was plenty of time. Technically, he had eight days of wiggle room. The storm wouldn't last eight days. The department of transportation crews wouldn't forget this road for eight days. There was no reason to be concerned about being stranded for a day or two. Particularly since he already had the check in hand.

Thinking about the check made him reach for his backpack. His partner wasn't involved in his family's feud, so Cooper had taken it upon himself to find the money for the balance of the mortgage. He'd cashed in his savings account and IRA, and had been forced to use the herd money, but he had almost every dime. All he needed was the pay from this delivery to add to the certified check. Then his brothers couldn't hurt him anymore. He'd never again be so stupid as to give them an opportunity like a mortgage to find him.

He unlatched the closure of the backpack, lifted the lid and slid his hand inside to get the white envelope containing the check he'd had prepared at the bank. When his fingers found only two sandwiches, a coffee Thermos and a Twix bar, his heart stopped and he dumped the contents of his backpack on the bed.

But as everything came tumbling out, he remembered he had put the check in the safe in his truck. A new kind of panic tightened his chest. But he reminded himself the truck was locked. Hell, the safe was locked and it was hidden, camouflaged as the seat back. On top of that, conditions outside weren't fit for man or beast. Nobody was going anywhere near his truck. His money was fine. There was absolutely no reason to freak out.

He sighed. He might not freak out, but he sure as hell couldn't feel comfortable about leaving a check worth hundreds of thousands of dollars in an abandoned vehicle. Still, since there was nothing he could do about that until morning, there was no sense dwelling on it.

After eating his sandwiches and returning the candy bar to his backpack, he lay down on the bed and angled his Stetson over his eyes, but from downstairs he heard the baby cry. The sound got louder and louder until little Daphne was screaming, sounding like she was testing out her lungs.

Cooper squeezed his eyes shut. Great. As if it wasn't bad enough he had a constant niggle of doubt about whether his check was safe, he was stuck with an over-sensitive woman and a crying baby. If he had any tolerance for cold at all, he'd go back to his truck, get his money and find another cabin.

But he couldn't handle the cold and it was getting dark, too dangerous to go outside even for a few minutes. He took a breath, pretending he couldn't hear the crying baby or the soothing voice of her mom and that he truly believed no one would steal his money, but he knew it would be a long, long night.

When Cooper opened his eyes again, muted light was edging into his bedroom through the dusty blinds on the window, and he bounced up in bed. He'd chosen this room for the thick comforter, but had drifted to sleep on top of the covers and spent the night without it.

He couldn't believe he'd fallen into such a deep slumber that he hadn't heard a screaming baby. Positive that something had happened—like maybe the storm had stopped and his roomie had gotten curious about what he had in his truck—Cooper rolled out of bed, bounded down the stairs and made the sharp left into the kitchen.

Zoe stood at the sink, washing dishes. Without turning around she said, "Don't worry. I didn't run out to your truck and plunder for valuables. The baby's just asleep."

He stiffened. The clock on the stove said seven-fifteen. It had only been light for about twenty minutes. If she'd gone to his truck, she'd still be shivering. His check was safe.

But her reply reminded him that she was one incredibly defensive lady. He couldn't even give her her privacy the night before without her jumping him about his motives. She might be among the world's most beautiful women but she was pricklier than a cactus and suspicious as hell. And if he didn't say something, he would alert her that there really was something of value in his truck.

"I wasn't worried."

"Sure you were. That's the only explanation for why you ran down the stairs like your feet were on fire." She paused, then added, "Unless there's no bathroom upstairs."

Confused, Cooper said, "I didn't see a bathroom."

"Well, there's a bathroom in the bedroom I'm using. It's the only one I found. This is a really old house. I'm guessing it was built before indoor plumbing because the bathroom was built in the corner of the bedroom."

Cooper suddenly understood what she was talking about. He'd been so focused on making sure she hadn't gone to his truck that he'd forgotten nature's call. He said, "Thanks," and left the room.

Glad for a few seconds to collect himself before he faced Madam Cactus again, Cooper conceded that he had all but told her he had something important in his truck. That meant at some point he would have to brave the storm, get his check and pin it in his underwear for safekeeping because he was absolutely positive that was one place she wouldn't look.

But after he stepped into her bedroom he forgot all about the check, the temperatures and even nature's call. He could smell her. He didn't know if she had special soap or shampoo or maybe perfume that she carried in her purse, but the room already smelled intimately of something light and tropical. Oceans and coconut oil. Suntan lotion.

His mind jumped to a hot beach and Zoe in a bikini and he squeezed his eyes shut. But he forced them open again. He was not attracted to her…well, he was attracted, but he knew he shouldn't be and he wasn't giving in to this…this…base instinct.

So, he held his breath as he quietly slid around the bed and into the small bathroom, which—just as she said—was built in the corner of the bedroom. He left as quickly as he could but as soon as he walked into the kitchen, the scent found him again because she was wearing it. As she stood at the sink, with her back to him, his gaze slid down the sleek locks of her pretty yellow hair, down her slim back, along the dip of her waist to her perfectly rounded backside, showcased in tight jeans.

Turning from the sink, she said, "There's bacon on the table."

Her silky blond hair curved around her cheeks and chin and then fell in lazy curls to a point somewhere between her collarbone and her breasts. When his gaze reached the bottom of the very last curl, he had to fight his eyes to move upward again.

"You found bacon?"

If Zoe noticed the way he had ogled her, she didn't let on. "There's plenty of food in the cupboards. Even meat and bread in the freezer."

After her reaction to being in someone's house the night before, that cheerful observation surprised him. "You looked around?"

She sighed. "I have a baby. I have to care for her. I had to see what was available and what wasn't. Besides, I've been up since five. Daphne went back to sleep but I couldn't, so I explored. You were right when you guessed this was a weekend retreat. But it's not for hunters. I think it belongs to a family. Though there's a poker table in the corner of the great room, the games in the cupboard are actually kids' games like 'Candyland' and 'Yahtzee.'"

She dried her hands on a dish towel and walked past him. Not giving him a chance to comment on her discovery, she said, "If you don't like bacon, there's sausage in the freezer. Make anything you want. I intend to leave cash on the table to pay for everything we use."

With that she walked out of the room and into the bedroom. She closed the door, effectively shutting him out the way he had shut her out the night before.

He shook his head in wonder, not sure if he was more surprised by her sense of responsibility or by the fact that she clearly wanted nothing to do with him.

Well, whatever. She couldn't have missed the way he'd taken inventory as if *she* were the breakfast buffet, so he didn't fault her for wanting to get away from him. He should be happy she'd removed the temptation of her fabulous face and figure. More than that, he should be absolutely joyful that she was making reparation for the bacon and bread. If she couldn't take a couple of food items without a conscience flare-up, he didn't have to worry that she would run to his truck and steal his money.

He grabbed two slices of bread, piled bacon on one and used the other for a lid, making himself a sandwich, and walked to the sink where he looked out the window at the storm.

He didn't even bother trying to stifle his groan. He could actually see the wind because it was picking up the icy snow pellets and tossing them around, as if the falling snow wasn't creating enough havoc on its own. That certainly proved there was no need for him to brave the elements to get his check. If there was anybody outside, they weren't plundering trucks. They were racing for shelter. As long as the wind wailed and the snow fell, his money was safe.

He ambled into the great room. A sofa and chair sat in front of the fireplace along the back wall. He saw the poker table Zoe had mentioned in the far corner. But he was more interested in the television.

He walked over, fell into one of the chairs in front of the TV and grabbed the remote from the end table. He pushed the power button and the screen came to life.

He almost hooted with joy. Not just entertainment, but satellite TV! In a few flicks of the remote he found sports, movies, reruns of old sitcoms. With something to do other than snipe at each other, he and Zoe could be in the same room.

Not that he wanted to be in the same room with her. He didn't. He simply didn't want to force her to stay behind a closed door with nothing to do, as if she were in prison.

But he also didn't want to give her the wrong impression about the two of them spending time together. If he invited her into the great room now, with the promise of television, it wouldn't appear he had changed his mind from the night before and now wanted to chitchat. His invitation would be to watch TV.

He bounced up from his seat. Sandwich in his left hand, he tapped on her bedroom door with his right. "Hey, the television works. If you want to come out and watch TV that would be cool. I wouldn't mind that."

"Thanks, but I'm going to take a shower."

Shower?

Instantly a vision of Zoe naked popped into his head. He could see her glorious yellow hair cascading around her. Her perfect pink skin. Her shining blue eyes. Her nice round…

He squeezed his eyes shut. He would like to blame that quick mental image on her for saying the word shower. But he knew hormones or maybe his gender were at fault. Still, smart men didn't chase after every good-looking woman they saw. They reminded themselves they were adults and also reminded themselves of all the reasons they couldn't act like sex-crazed teenagers. Lord knows, he'd fought this battle before. He'd simply used logic and proper behavior. And this time around he had plenty of ammo.

First, he didn't want anything to do with this woman. Second, she sure as hell didn't want anything to do with him. And third, he had TV. There was absolutely no reason to stand outside her bedroom door salivating.

He said, "Okay. Great," then could have kicked himself because the way he'd said it he sounded as if he thought the idea of her taking a shower was great. Well, too late to fix that. Time to retreat and hope for the best.

He nearly ran back to the great room, shoving the remainder of his sandwich into his mouth before he picked up the remote. He clicked through the unfamiliar stations until he found the Weather Channel then wished he hadn't.

Staring at the map of the United States, he moaned in frustration. The storm that had stranded them had stalled over the mountain. The forecaster happily expected it to move on by the next morning. But *he* could be happy about that because he wasn't stranded with a woman he didn't know and her baby. The weatherman also didn't have a check representing every cent he had in the safe of his abandoned truck!

A half hour later, Zoe came into the great room dressed in brown pants and a soft-looking red sweater, holding a happy Daphne. Though Cooper didn't really want to make small talk, the obvious observation came out before he could stop it.

"Looks like you're the same size as the woman of the house."

"I wouldn't know. There are no clothes in the closet. I keep an extra pair of pants and a sweater in the diaper bag because babies are messy and sometimes I end up needing changing as much as Daphne."

She turned toward the kitchen and Cooper's gaze took in every inch of her perfect body. A million visions and images popped into his head. Once again he blamed his hormones. Once again he knew logic and proper behavior would keep him in line. He forced his gaze upward away from her backside, but when he did he saw the way her pale curls contrasted with her sexy red sweater and a whole bunch of other images sprang to his mind.

He rubbed his hand along his nape. Did the woman own any color except red? Sure, she looked great in red, but that was the problem. She looked too damned great. Too damned sexy.

Taking himself back to logic and proper behavior again, he reminded himself that even if she found him as attractive as he found her, they couldn't sleep together. They were stranded for two days. If it were only for the afternoon, a fling wouldn't be out of the question. But two days didn't work. If he seduced her, sex wouldn't last two days. Eventually, they'd stop and she'd want to talk and then they'd know too much about each other. And then it wouldn't be a fling. It would be the beginning of a relationship.

His stomach knotted. No way.

"I'm afraid I have some bad news."

"Storm's getting worse," Zoe said, turning to face him, and Cooper's stomach plummeted.

She was darned gorgeous. He couldn't believe any man was capable of speech around her, let alone capable of leaving her once he married her. Then he realized she had to be a shrew for her husband to have left her. So far her behavior around him sort of hinted to that. Even the way she always had to be one step ahead of him was an indication that she needed to be right.

No man liked that kind of one-upmanship in a woman. Hell, no man liked that in another man.

He drew a quick breath. "Well, excuse me for trying to help."

Zoe had been on her way to the kitchen again to take one of Daphne's bottles out of the fridge where she had stored them the night before, but his comment stopped her. She wasn't sure why he thought she was simple-minded or stupid, but she knew from their conversation the night before that he worried that she would be a burden. She'd thought she'd already put that doubt to bed, but apparently he was still skeptical.

"I found the TV, too," she added.

"I was just trying to tell you about the storm."

There was that tone again. As if she were an idiot. This guy might be the sexiest man on the face of the earth with his whipcord-lean body very nicely show-cased in his worn workshirt and perfect-fitting jeans. Add his silky-looking black hair, and she couldn't pretend that she didn't notice his physical attributes. But he also had chauvinist written all over him and she simply wasn't putting up with it.

"Here's the deal, Bryant," she said, deliberately using his last name to keep them on totally impersonal terms, so he could stop treating her as if she were a ninny. "I have a child. I don't just pay my own way. I also pay hers because my ex doesn't believe in child support. No matter how many court orders get issued, if he runs fast enough he can always evade them. So, I work. I take care of a household. I can fix a faucet. I can fix a tire. I can make a fire. I can turn on a TV."

"Very funny."

"No. It's not funny. It's not one damned bit funny that I have to tell you I'm a capable adult because you clearly think I'm some kind of spoiled princess or something. I'd like to get that squared away so we can move on."

"We can move on."

"Great. Because if we're stuck here for the weekend I don't intend to be the only one cooking and doing the dishes."

"That's fine by me because, just like you, I work and take care of my own house…and run a ranch." He smiled tightly. "I guess you could say I have you beat."

She turned to go into the kitchen again. "You won't have me beat until you also add in caring for a child."

He followed her. "Last year, three of my cows had calves."

She slammed the refrigerator closed. "Did you have to get up with them at two in the morning?"

"Once. And I'm painfully familiar with colic."

"Well, good for you. You're the first man I consider myself equal to."

His eyes narrowed as if he knew she'd insulted him—or somebody—but he couldn't figure out how. Zoe took Daphne and her bottle into the great room. She settled on the rocking chair and fed the baby one of the five bottles of formula she had prepared the night before. Even if they could leave tomorrow, and she knew they couldn't, Daphne would be out of bottles before that. Zoe would have to again prepare formula from the faucet water and there was no guarantee that wouldn't eventually upset Daphne's system.

Preoccupied with the baby, Zoe didn't notice that an uncomfortable silence had settled over the small house or that Cooper Bryant was pacing until Daphne had fallen asleep and Zoe rose from the rocker to take the baby into the bedroom. Even then, she didn't say anything. It was not her problem that Cooper Bryant was pacing the room, obviously bored.

She laid Daphne in the center of the double bed and began to arrange the pillows around her. But, on second thought, she pushed the bed against the wall, giving Daphne two sides of protection. It wasn't the best situation in the world, but they were stranded. As long as Zoe checked on the baby every few minutes, Daphne should be fine.

Satisfied, Zoe ambled into the great room. She wasn't

much for TV, but she had seen a deck of cards. It had been a while since she'd played solitaire. Entertaining herself that way would be fun. In fact, it was a great deal of fun to be away from her house that always needed to be cleaned, the mountain of bills she couldn't pay and the notice that told her her house was going up for sheriff's sale because no one had paid the taxes.

She entered the great room and found Cooper Bryant staring out the French doors behind the poker table. If it weren't for *him,* this weekend away from reality might actually be a nice break.

He didn't turn from staring at the mounting snow, which Zoe had earlier watched just as he was doing right now. She was sure the look of disbelief on his face probably mirrored the one she'd worn staring at the sight.

Approaching the poker table, Zoe said nothing. She opened the top drawer of a cabinet, found the cards, pulled a chair away from the table and sat. The only sound in the room was the noise the cards made as they slid against each other when she shuffled.

"I'm not much of a card player."

"Great. I was going to play solitaire."

He turned. Crossing his arms on his chest he said, "Okay. I *get* it. I get it big-time. You are not a helpless female who needs someone to take care of her."

She began to lay out the cards. "Thanks for recognizing the obvious."

He scowled and Zoe dropped the cards and studied him for a second before she said, "Look, I know you'd rather be alone. Frankly, so would I. But since we aren't, the alternative for us is to form some kind of a truce."

"A truce?"

"Sure. We agree to share chores. We agree to be civil. And we declare each other off-limits romantically. That way, we can talk pleasantly without worrying that one or the other is getting any ideas."

Because what she said made sense, Cooper almost agreed until a tantalizing thought entered his head. Whether she knew it or not she had just backhandedly admitted that she found him attractive, too. They were stuck together. They were both attracted. Neither one of them wanted a relationship with the other.

This weekend could be a lot of fun if he could figure out a way to convince her that they should take advantage of their two days away from real life by having a bit of no-strings-attached sex.

But before he could come up with a way to form the suggestion, Daphne cried and Zoe was off her chair and in the bedroom like a bolt of lightning. Cooper realized *that* was the reason he and Zoe couldn't have no-strings-attached sex. Women with babies had a guaranteed, built-in defense mechanism. Every time things heated up, Daphne would probably start crying.

Zoe came out of the bedroom carrying Daphne. The baby looked tired, but not sleepy, and though Cooper knew little to nothing about kids, he didn't think this was a good sign. Zoe didn't say a word. She simply walked back to the table, sat on the chair, put the baby on her lap, and continued her solitaire game.

Cooper turned to look at the snow again. "I think a truce is a good idea."

"Okay. Great. Now we can be civil."

He nodded and relaxed a little, but not completely. He may no longer fear that she wanted something from him, but that didn't stop his sexual attraction. Because he was a responsible adult he would curb it, but controlling it required being wise about distance and proximity, and also being careful about the conversational topics he chose.

Luckily, the weather was always safe. "I've never seen snow fall like this before."

"I have. A few times." She paused, then said, "Daphne, honey, don't grab the cards."

Cooper faced the table again. Zoe held the baby on her lap with one arm and used the other hand to grasp Daphne's little fingers to keep them away from the cards.

She smiled up at him. "Would it be out of line for me to ask you to put that red seven on that black eight?"

He glanced down, saw the play she mentioned, and shifted the seven of hearts to the eight of spades.

"Thanks."

"You're welcome." He almost turned again to the window, but courtesy wouldn't let him. "Want the red four on the black five?"

"What red four?"

"This one," he said, taking the card from its spot on the board and placing it on the five.

"Oh. Didn't see that. Thanks."

He took a seat across the table, grabbed the card stack, and asked, "Do you play one card at a time or three?"

"Three."

"Do you shuffle them or play them in order?"

She gave him a horrified look. "I play them in order. Anything else is trying to beat the odds! I play fair."

He stifled a smile. This woman had some set of morals. "Okay. Whatever." He counted off three cards and placed them face up so she could see her play options.

She sighed. "That card goes nowhere. Try again."

He counted off the next three cards and slapped them on the table.

"Oh, an ace!" She glanced at him. "You know where that goes."

He stifled another smile at her enthusiasm and put the ace of spades at the top of her play area. He jutted his chin toward the cards on the table. "Want that two of spades up here?"

She nodded, but said nothing else as she examined the board. Daphne screeched, trying to pull her hand free of Zoe's.

"If I let your hand go," Zoe said to her baby, "will you promise not to touch the cards?"

Daphne only screeched again.

"I'm not sure I'd take that as a yes," Cooper cautioned and the little girl grinned toothlessly at him. She was an adorable kid. Her eyes were big and blue, like her mom's, and her hair was so light it sometimes looked white.

"I agree. But I can't sit here holding her hand all morning. It's probably driving her crazy." She released Daphne's hand and the little girl instantly pounded it on the table.

Cooper began sliding the cards in play away from Daphne and closer to himself. He was surprised that he only had to move them three inches to get them out of her reach.

Zoe smiled her thanks.

Cooper's heart did a somersault. It was so damned

unfair to be alone in a cabin with a woman this good-looking and not be able to even *try* to seduce her.

"You're a natural at handling babies."

He cleared his throat. "Like I said, I did have those three calves last year."

She laughed. Cooper counted out three more cards and set them on the growing stack.

"Put that red nine on the black ten."

He did as she asked.

"Black eight on the red nine," she said with a nod toward the card. He made the move.

Studying the board, looking for additional plays, she said, "So, you own a ranch."

He realized he'd set himself up for the question since his ranch was the only thing he'd spoken about and the only conversational opening she had. But the last thing he wanted to talk about was the ranch. It only reminded him that he was forking out his herd money because his brothers hated him.

Unfortunately, he couldn't ignore her when they'd finally found a way to be amiable. "Yeah. I own a ranch."

"And you drive a truck?"

"Yeah."

"So who watches the calves while you're away?"

"They're not exactly like Daphne. I don't have to put them in day care."

She nodded. "So you just leave everything alone, jump in your truck and go?"

"No. It's not that easy, either."

Daphne patted Zoe's face and screeched. Zoe caught her hand. "Would you mind…" She sighed. "No. Forget it. I'll do it."

"Do what?"

"Get a rattle from her diaper bag," Zoe said, but she rose and began walking toward the bedroom where he knew she had stashed the baby's things. When she returned, Daphne was chewing on something that looked like a blue plastic pretzel.

"I could have gotten that."

Zoe shook her head. "Right."

"Are you back to showing me how strong you are?"

She glanced at him. "I don't know. Are you going to tell me who babysits your cows?"

"You're basing how you react to me on the fact that I didn't tell you I have a partner?"

"I'm basing how I treat you on how you treat me. You'll help with my card game because you're bored, but you won't tell me about your life—even the insignificant fact that you have a partner—because you don't trust me. And since you don't trust me, that makes you suspicious. People are typically suspicious of other people because they aren't trustworthy themselves…. So…" She shrugged. "I didn't think it wise to let you rummage through my stuff."

He stared at her. "Are you kidding me? You think I'm some kind of criminal because I won't tell you about myself?"

She shrugged. "No, I just don't think you're trustworthy."

"I'm one of the most trustworthy people on the face of the earth!"

"Yeah. Right. That's why you're so suspicious."

"I'm *not* suspicious. I'm simply not much of a people person."

She didn't answer, only stared at him until he couldn't take it anymore and said, "What?"

"I'm waiting for you to tell me why you're not a people person."

He laughed. "Why should I?"

"Oh, come on. We're here in the middle of a snowstorm. Nine chances out of ten when we get out of here Monday, we'll never see each other again. This is like a fantasy or something. It's our one chance to pour our hearts out to a member of the opposite sex and get some answers."

He stared at her. "*That* is your *fantasy.*"

She was silent for a minute, then she said, "Well, I never actually thought of it as a fantasy, per se. But I have thought that just once I would like to sit a man down and ask him some pointed questions so I can figure out what the hell makes your gender tick."

"Well, honey, I've got a fantasy, too. And it also involves being stranded with a member of the opposite sex. And we communicate, too. Except we don't talk. We communicate on that extraspecial level that doesn't require talking. You know what I'm saying?"

Her eyes narrowed. "You want me to have sex with you?"

He smiled.

"A stranger?" she said, horrified.

"Women." He laughed and shook his head. "Look, honey, it's every bit as preposterous for me to pour my heart out to someone I don't know as it is for you to have sex with someone you don't know." He shoved his chair away from the table and started toward the kitchen. "I'm going to make another pot of coffee," he said, but he stopped suddenly because something she'd said had finally penetrated his thick brain. They really wouldn't see each other after the snowplow went through. Monday morning when they parted company, it would be as if they had never met. He could tell her every damned tidbit and morsel about his life and it wouldn't matter.

In fact, it was beginning to sound like a nice compromise. And why shouldn't it? She wanted to talk. He wanted to spend the weekend engaged in a more pleasurable pursuit.

They could both get what they wanted.

He faced her. "You know what? I really would like for you to think about my offer. No. Let's call it a proposition. If you agree to spend Daphne's next nap having no-strings-attached sex with me, I'll talk your ear off. I'll tell you absolutely everything you want to know." He stopped and grinned. "And here's a teaser. I haven't spoken with my brothers in eight years. They recently bought the mortgage to my ranch and they are foreclosing."

Zoe blinked at him.

"The story behind all this is rich and juicy…" He smiled again. "Curious?"

Chapter Three

God help her, she *was* curious. But not curious enough to have sex with a stranger. That was simply a ridiculous suggestion, even if she had experienced a zing of sexual awareness when he'd said it.

Not because he was good-looking. Physical attractiveness might be part of the reason she reacted to Cooper Bryant, but it was the ease with which he slid them into a negotiation for what he wanted that caused her blood to heat in her veins. He had no compunction about going after what he wanted. He wanted her. He said it. He negotiated for it. After months of focusing only on caring for her baby, having a man behave so boldly was a stark reminder that she had more facets to her personality than simply being a mother. She was also a woman. No matter how outrageous his suggestion, it was still flattering.

She shivered and decided she'd simply been without

male attention for too long and told herself to stop thinking with her hormones. Particularly since she suspected he'd been either trying to shut her up or joking when he'd made his suggestion. Except she didn't think he'd been kidding about his family. The words had come out too quickly for him to make them up on the spur of the moment. She would bet her last fifty cents there really was a story there.

And she intended to get it. Not so much because she was nosy as bored. Plus, his mentioning his family might have been a subconscious clue that he *needed* to talk. Otherwise, he wouldn't have brought them up. Because she didn't think it was possible for anybody to be trapped with another person for two days and not talk, she knew she could get this story out of him. In fact, she decided to make it a game. Having a purpose to the long, empty hours that stretched ahead of them was a much better way to pass the time than playing cards.

She considered for a second that initiating any kind of cat-and-mouse game with him might be dangerous. His additional life experience probably made him quicker, sharper than she was. Worse, if he hadn't been joking when he'd made his suggestion, he'd very clearly told her what he wanted in exchange for his story. If she wasn't careful, she might find herself in *his* trap.

Nah. He wasn't *that* clever. And she was a lot smarter than people believed a blonde could be. She would know if she was getting herself in over her head and she would simply drop back.

While Cooper made the coffee, Zoe fed Daphne the remains of her bottle and the little girl fell asleep. Though Zoe's daughter typically didn't take a nap after every bottle, today Daphne seemed listless and cranky. Zoe gently set the sleeping baby in the middle of the bed and Daphne didn't stir. Curious, Zoe sat beside her. After a close inspection, she noticed the Daphne's cheeks were a brighter pink than usual. She placed her palm on the baby's forehead and realized she had a fever.

Having been a mother for six months, Zoe didn't panic. She had a thermometer and a bottle of pain reliever/fever reducer in her diaper bag. She would use one to find out if she needed the other. She rose from the bed and rummaged through the baby things until she found both and set them on the dresser for easy access when Daphne woke up.

Then she stood by the bed, not quite sure what to do.

There weren't many options in a house in the woods during a storm. With Daphne asleep, Zoe's only choice was to go out to the great room. But then she would be tempted to talk to Cooper and that wasn't a good idea. She didn't want to talk too much or too soon. He would recognize she was digging and he would clam up. Or, worse, remind her of his proposition. If getting him to open up was going to be the big weekend challenge that kept her from dying of boredom, she had to be smart about it.

At the same time, she couldn't stay in the bedroom as if she were afraid of him. That could make him believe he had the upper hand and every time he wanted something, all he would have to do would be suggest they sleep together. The trick to getting Cooper's family secret would be balance. Casualness. She had to project an attitude that said she was comfortable with him but not overly interested. Eventually, out of sheer boredom he would reveal a bit here and a piece there, and pretty soon, he would have confided his whole sordid tale.

That sounded like the perfect way to handle her challenge, so Zoe cast one more glance at sleeping Daphne. The baby appeared peaceful, but she wouldn't be asleep forever. When she awakened, probably achy and miserable if she had caught a virus, Daphne would be whiny and weepy and Zoe would have to dedicate her full attention to her.

Best to get into the great room now while she had some time and start making friends so she could get Cooper Bryant's story.

With one last peek at Daphne, Zoe left the bedroom and strolled into the great room. Cooper had pushed the two TV chairs out of the way and replaced them with the sofa where he currently lay watching television.

"What's on?"

"Basketball." He gave her a pained look that somehow made him look extremely masculine and sexy. "You're not going to ask me to change channels, are you?"

Telling herself to stop noticing how sexy he was, she glanced at the screen. Sports. She'd simply never found a way to get interested in them. But she wasn't the type of person to begrudge another of his pleasure. Besides, letting him have this favor was a great way to begin showing him she was kind and trustworthy—somebody he could talk to.

She smiled at Cooper, as one friend smiled at another. "No, you watch. I'm fine. I can play solitaire."

Without acknowledging her warm expression in any

way, Cooper settled into the sofa and glued his gaze to the screen. He didn't so much as grunt a thanks.

Well, whatever. Part of gaining his trust was not pushing for an answer when he didn't believe any was required. She had to show him she accepted him as he was so he would feel comfortable telling her his big juicy life secret.

She sat at the poker table and saw that her original solitaire game hadn't been disturbed. She resumed play and within three or four moves realized that the game was lost. She gathered the cards and started again. Within a few plays, though, that game was lost, too. So she gathered, dealt and started again. Another loser. Another deal. Another loss. Deal. Loss. Deal. Loss.

She squeezed her eyes shut. She didn't mind being unlucky, but being unlucky while bored could drive anyone insane.

She glanced longingly at the television, then at Cooper. Were his eyes closed?

She slowly rose from the poker table and walked to the head of the sofa. Peering down, she confirmed that his eyes were tightly shut and realized he wasn't *watching* the game. He was *sleeping through* the game.

Unfortunately, he was also holding the remote. On his stomach. Right about belt level.

After all the reactions she'd been having to him since he'd made his preposterous proposition, she wasn't sure touching him in any way, shape or form was wise. But the man *was* sleeping and she wanted the TV.

Studying the perfect male specimen stretched out before her, Zoe got another of those zings of attraction. He was solid man. Somebody who worked for his muscles, didn't just work out. In his jeans and plaid shirt he was nothing but pure, unadulterated man. He was so gorgeous *any* woman would have reactions to him.

Which meant she was perfectly normal, and she shouldn't be making a big deal out of simply taking the remote from his hand. Because it wasn't a big deal. He was attractive and she noticed. So what? It wasn't as if the remote was on his upper thigh. It was on his stomach. No big deal.

Slowly, quietly, she reached down, loosely gripped the top of the remote and began sliding it from his hold. But before it was even halfway out, his free hand came up and clamped around her wrist.

Without opening his eyes he said, "If you're taking me up on my proposition, I want to be awake for that. Actually, I think I *need* to be awake for that."

Heart racing, Zoe snatched her wrist from his grasp and jumped back. "I wasn't taking you up on your proposition! I want the remote."

"You said I could watch television."

"Yeah, but then you fell asleep…" Damn it! Her heart wouldn't slow down. Her limbs were trembling. He'd just about scared her lungs into collapsing.

"I wasn't asleep. I was listening to the game."

"Right," she scoffed.

"I really was," he said, then gave her the exact score.

Because basketball was a game where points could be added in a matter of seconds, she knew he wasn't lying and, chastising herself for having any kind of attraction to such an idiot, she went back to the poker table. Before she sat, however, she heard Daphne stir so she changed direction and went to check on her.

As Zoe entered the bedroom, Daphne opened her eyes and Zoe saw they were glassy. Combining the look in Daphne's eyes with her now bright red cheeks could have been enough to confirm that she had a fever, but wanting to be safe rather than sorry, Zoe took the thermometer to check Daphne's exact temperature. Sure enough, it was above normal. Not high enough to worry, but high enough to warrant medicine.

After setting the thermometer on the dresser again, Zoe reached down to lift the baby from the center of the double bed and turned toward the door. Grabbing the medicine with her free hand, she headed for the kitchen. Apparently dazed from her virus, Daphne didn't even whimper until Zoe slid the teaspoon of liquid medicine on her tongue, then her lips trembled and she opened her mouth to protest and a red stream of fever reducer poured from each corner.

"It's okay, Daphne. You're going to be fine." Zoe used the teaspoon to gather the medicine from the baby's chin and force it back into her mouth, but by this time Daphne was crying in earnest and the liquid came sputtering out again.

It took three tries, but eventually Zoe was satisfied with the amount of medicine Daphne had swallowed and she cuddled the baby against her chest, rocking her back and forth.

"It's okay, sweetie. Mommy knows you don't feel well. Just give the medicine a few minutes and you'll go to sleep again."

Daphne cried harder. Zoe began pacing the kitchen, rocking, cooing soothing words. But nothing helped and before Zoe could prevent it, Daphne began to scream.

Cooper sat up on the couch. "Are you beating her?"

Zoe sighed. "No." She paused, considering whether or not she should tell him her daughter had caught a virus—which meant he had been exposed to a virus—and decided she might as well. In these close quarters, there would be very few secrets from him.

"Daphne must have caught a virus at day care."

Cooper looked at Zoe for a few seconds as she stood in the hall between the kitchen and the great room, rocking the sobbing infant.

"So this is what I have to look forward to for the next few days?"

"No, only a couple of hours," Zoe guessed. "If it's a twenty-four-hour bug she may have had symptoms I didn't notice last night." She drew a quick breath. "So, she could be over this in twelve hours or so."

Cooper frowned and said, "If you're worried about me, don't. I've made the best of worse situations before." Then he lay down on the sofa again.

"I'm not worried about you. I'm worried about her."

He sat up again. "Don't worry about her, either. My mom always taught me that you shouldn't borrow trouble. Do you have a thermometer in that trash can of yours?"

"Yes. I already took her temp. It was a little high."

"Does she feel like she's burning up?"

"No. She's hot but she's not burning up."

He smiled patiently. "Okay, then. Your thermometer's probably right. She has a temperature, but it's not too high. No borrowing trouble."

As he said the last, Zoe noticed that Daphne was no longer crying. Her eyelids were droopy, her cheeks still bore two round red spots and she gave her mother a pitiful look.

"Mommy's going to take you to bed," Zoe said as she carried Daphne to the bedroom. She laid her among the pillows but instead of leaving her, Zoe lay down, too. She rubbed the baby's arms, smoothed her hair, whispered soothing words. In twenty minutes, probably the time it took for the fever reducer to kick in, Daphne was sleeping again.

Though Zoe rose from the bed, she couldn't seem to pull herself out of the bedroom. She knew Cooper was correct. Daphne's fever wasn't so high that her life was in danger, but Zoe didn't want to leave her just in case. Because there was no chair in the room, she sat on the floor and propped her back against the wall. She sat, staring straight ahead and listened to the sounds of Daphne breathing.

Twenty minutes later Cooper appeared at the bedroom door. "What's up?"

"Nothing. She's sleeping."

"Game's not over, but it's getting dull, so if you'd like to watch TV, I'll find something else to do."

From her position on the floor, Zoe smiled up at him. "No. I'm fine. I need to be here, just in case."

Cooper turned to leave, but his face pinched with a pained expression and he stopped halfway and sighed. "My mother used to do the same thing."

"Sit in your bedroom when you were sick?"

"I don't remember her doing it for me, but I remember she did it for my baby brother, Seth. So, I assume she did it for all of us."

"That's right. You said you have brothers."

He hesitated. "Two."

"I'm an only child." She paused. "It must have been fun to have siblings."

"Don't try to slide me into a conversation thinking I'll spill my guts about my family. You know the deal on getting my story."

She laughed. "I wasn't trying to get your story."

"Good, because I would have made a great spy. I don't tell anyone anything."

"Except in return for sex."

"Everybody's got his price."

She laughed again and Cooper left the room. But he felt guilty and he didn't know why. He hadn't made Zoe's kid sick. But he didn't have a clue how to help, either. And for some reason known only to God, he felt he should be doing something.

Seeing that it was close to noon, he decided to make lunch. As a fresh pot of coffee brewed, he threw together some sandwiches using one of several cans of tuna he found in a lower cabinet. He took two sandwiches and a cup of coffee to the bedroom.

"Here."

She glanced up and Cooper's heart turned over in his chest. Her eyes were such a soft shade of blue that they could zap the strength of any mere mortal man. But this was the first time he'd really looked at her face and seen something more appealing than just attractiveness. He saw strength, grit, determination. All the stuff that when used in the right way, at the right time, could make a woman incredibly good in bed.

His gut tightened and if he had had a free hand he would have slapped himself upside of the head. What was he doing thinking about her like that? It was one thing to proposition her. It was quite another to torture himself.

He shoved the plate and cup at her.

She shook her head. "I'm not hungry."

"Well, eat to keep from getting bored then."

"That's how people get fat."

She wouldn't take the dish. He couldn't seem to get himself out of the room unless she did. Damn attraction! Damn woman!

"All right," he said and lowered himself to the floor. "Here's the deal. I'm not much of a people person. I shouldn't give a darn about you, but for some reason I cannot fathom, it's driving me nuts having you in here."

Zoe studied him for a second, then shrugged. "I don't see why. You would have let me sit at the poker table with nothing to do. How's it different to have me in here?"

He scowled at her perceptiveness. "I don't know." He picked up a sandwich and took a bite. If she wasn't going to eat the damned sandwiches, he would. And once they were gone he wouldn't have any more reason to stay.

Zoe was quiet for another few seconds, then from the look on her face Cooper could tell she'd drawn some kind of conclusion. He wasn't a bit surprised when she said, "I think I know why it drives you nuts to have me in here." Apparently having changed her mind about the sandwiches, she lifted the second one from the plate. "When I was in the great room, you knew what I was doing. While I'm in here, you don't. You don't like to be left out."

He supposed it was because he'd just mentioned Seth's name, but in his head Cooper heard his younger brother say the same words eight years ago. *You don't like to be left out. You have to know everything. Even when you know as well as Ty knows that having you involved is going to cause trouble. It would be such a relief if you would just leave!*

As if it were yesterday, emotion rushed through Cooper. Fear. Pain. Pride. Anger. He remembered Seth had stormed out of the bedroom and Cooper had decided to oblige him and leave. He had packed in less time than most people took to change clothes and was gone before Seth could have second thoughts about what he'd said or Ty could realize his middle brother was heading out of town.

Not that he thought either of them would have stopped him, but at the time he had needed that sliver of doubt. He'd needed to believe they cared enough not to allow him to go and that he could only get out of town if no one knew he was going.

"I'm actually better on my own." He rose to leave, but Zoe gaped at him as if he were crazy.

"How can anybody be better off on their own? When I turned eighteen my parents divorced. I don't know how I missed it, but they were only staying together for me. *Me.*" She shook her head and looked at the ceiling. "Anyway, they got divorced and my mom moved to California where she hoped to get into movies and actually married an actor who does a lot of bit parts. My dad moved to Florida, where he fishes. The parents who were so careful to make sure I had a family left me totally without one, as if eighteen was some sort of magic number that made it okay."

Cooper said, "That's rough," but he didn't sit again.

Instead, he turned to the door. "If your coffee's cold there's a whole pot out here to refresh it with."

Zoe smiled ruefully and he knew she hadn't missed his not-too-subtle escape from their personal conversation. But he didn't care. His family was the last thing he wanted to think about. Unless she wanted to take him up on his proposition; then he would keep his end of the bargain and dredge up memories of how he and his brothers didn't get along. But Cooper didn't think she would sleep with him, so her virtue and his sanity were safe.

Zoe stayed in the bedroom another twenty minutes and though Cooper tried to watch TV, there was nothing interesting being shown. He walked to the French doors and stared at the falling snow for a few minutes. Paced for a few more. Turned off the coffeepot. Rinsed it out. Wiped down the countertop. Watched it snow some more.

Finally, he skulked over to the bedroom again. "Still asleep?"

"She whimpered a few times. I sung her back to sleep."

"I didn't hear you sing."

"Do you think I'm going to sing loud enough for you to hear?"

He grinned. "Is your voice that bad?"

"No. But baby songs aren't exactly top ten. I sing about bunnies and cats and puffy clouds that talk."

"Now, see. There might be some entertainment in that. Sing a bunny song."

She shook her head. "No."

"Sing about the puffy clouds then."

"No! I will not entertain you. Go watch TV."

Once again Cooper felt himself tumble back through time, and as if he were ten he heard his father say, *Go watch TV.* How many times had his parents said that? They'd regularly shoo him and his brothers to the television or to the store…anywhere so they could have peace and quiet. And Ty, Cooper and Seth would run outside and have a ball, probably making enough noise to wake the dead.

But Zoe hadn't had siblings. When her parents had said, "Go watch TV," she had been alone.

And she was alone now. Except for this baby. It was no wonder she was so protective of her.

"So what happened with your husband?"

She peered up, studied him for a few seconds, then sighed. "He left when I discovered I was pregnant."

"He didn't want kids?"

"He wanted to be successful first."

Cooper understood wanting to succeed. In his best daydreams he didn't as much as say hello to either of his brothers until he had proven himself. Which was why they were foreclosing on his ranch. For as much as he wanted to prove they were wrong—he wasn't a no-account troublemaker who would never amount to anything—they were determined to prove they were right. But as God was his witness, he would win that battle. He would prove himself.

She sighed. "I'm guessing you understand that, since you didn't say something sympathetic when I told you why he left."

Cooper licked his suddenly dry lips, then said the

only thing he could say. "I can't understand someone leaving his own child. But I do understand him wanting to achieve success. Sorry."

"It's all right. I know men and women are different. All I have to do is look at my parents to see that. She's in California drinking green tea and taking vitamins and my dad's in Florida swilling beer and wearing the same clothes for three days."

Cooper laughed. "Oh, come on."

"It's true. He's not much on laundry and he claims fish have no sense of smell."

"So you talk with him by phone?"

"When I can afford it." She paused. "He doesn't call me."

Inwardly, Cooper groaned. Zoe Montgomery was pretty, sweet and the most devoted mother he'd ever seen, yet she'd been treated abysmally. If he didn't at least dole out one line of commiseration, he would be no better than the mother, father and husband who had left her.

"Men aren't much for talking."

She laughed quietly. "No kidding."

He took a breath, deciding this would be a nice time to leave the room, but before he could she said, "So what are your parents like?"

"My parents were nice," he said, "but they were killed in an automobile accident."

Clearly mortified by her mistake, she gasped, "Oh, God! I'm so sorry."

"It's all right. It was years ago."

"And now your brothers are taking the family ranch and cheating you out of your share of the inheritance?"

He grimaced. "No. My brothers and I were raised in a tiny town in Arkansas. My parents owned a small construction company that came to us when they died. I bought the ranch in Texas a few years after I left home." He paused, then added, "Technically, I walked out on my share of the inheritance a long time ago. They didn't cheat me out of it."

She stared at him, obviously waiting for him to continue. He said nothing.

"You're really not going to tell me why, are you?"

"You know my price."

"Right."

"Besides, you've already gotten more out of me than most people." Without a pause, he changed the subject. "What do you want for supper?"

It took her a second to catch up, but finally she said, "Didn't we just eat lunch?"

"Not much to do here. Besides, if we want roast or something, the meat will need time to thaw and bake. There are potatoes in the one cupboard. I can make mashed or baked or just plain buttered." He paused, then said, "Anything tempting you?"

"No. But I just ate." She waved her hand in dismissal. "Go cook, Chef Boyardee. Make whatever you want. I'm not picky."

He turned to leave, but Zoe called after him, "Hey, and check the Weather Channel again."

He grimaced. He knew why she wanted him to check the Weather Channel. She wanted to leave. Maybe to get Daphne to a doctor. Or maybe because he wasn't any more entertaining than she was. Of course, he grudgingly admitted, she was somewhat interesting. She had a sad life and she sang idiotic songs to the baby her husband hadn't wanted.

All right. So he was a bit curious.

Only a few minutes after Cooper left, Zoe decided she needed to move, too. With her behind numb from sitting on the hard floor, she had to roll to her side to rise. Daphne hadn't awakened or whimpered, but now Zoe herself was feeling somewhat tired. She blamed the cold, the boredom and her fitful sleep from the night before. She lay beside the baby and after only a few minutes her eyelids began to droop. She reminded herself that it would be a hell of boredom to be up all night because she'd taken a nap, but couldn't seem to force her eyes to stay open.

What felt like hours later, a knock awakened her. Disoriented, she glanced around the dark room and realized it was after five because the sun had set. She looked at Daphne, who was awake but still listless.

Cooper knocked again. "Is everything okay in there?"

Zoe said, "Yeah. We'll be out in a minute." She pushed herself off the bed and found a lamp to light the room before she grabbed Daphne and made her way to the door.

When she opened it, Cooper was standing there. "Kid okay?"

A bit groggy from her nap, Zoe nodded. "She's still sick. I have the medicine on the counter out here. After I try to get her to eat something, I'll give her another dose and she'll go back to sleep." She paused, then said, "Would you mind getting her baby seat and bringing the diaper bag out so I can get a jar of food?"

He said sure and Zoe started to feel guilty that she

had disliked him so much in the beginning. No matter what he said, he really wasn't as bad as he thought he was. Worse, she was also feeling a tad guilty that she still intended to pry his secret out of him. Of course, with Daphne sick, there might not be time for that. So, maybe there wasn't anything to feel guilty about.

He brought the baby seat to the kitchen. Zoe set it in the center of the table and strapped Daphne inside. Then she rummaged through the diaper bag for a jar of baby food. She chose apple, because it seemed to be the kind that would probably sit the easiest on the baby's stomach, opened it and got a spoon from the drawer by the sink.

Clearly bored to tears, Cooper Bryant had watched her every move. "That's all you do? Just open the jar and get a spoon?"

"Sometimes, if she's having a vegetable like strained carrots, I heat the food. But for applesauce, this is all I do." She spooned out a mouthful of food and put it to Daphne's lips. Daphne took the bite and swallowed it. Feeling victorious, Zoe scooped a second spoonful, but apparently the first hadn't set as well as Zoe had hoped and Daphne spat it out.

Zoe put the lid back on the jar and handed it to Cooper. "Put this in the refrigerator, would you?"

"That's it?"

"She's not hungry. She's got a virus. She probably can't even drink her formula. Once I give her some more medicine, I'm going to feed her a bottle of water and hope she goes back to sleep."

An hour later, Cooper tiptoed to Zoe's bedroom again and peeked inside. Not only had Daphne fallen asleep but Zoe had, too. He stretched into the room, reaching for the switch on the lamp and extinguished the light. Zoe may not want to go to bed at seven o'clock, but she was asleep so she might as well get some rest. She might be up the entire night if Daphne decided she was done sleeping.

When Cooper went to bed at ten, Zoe and Daphne hadn't stirred, but he heard them a few times in the course of the night. He couldn't really sleep, and when he did drift off he had odd dreams, mostly about his family. He didn't care to remember the good times and he sure as hell didn't want to relive the bad, so when his wristwatch said six, he rolled out of bed. He didn't know if Zoe had heated any of the dinner he'd prepared the day before, but because she had rocked a baby all night he decided she needed nourishment.

He slipped downstairs and into the kitchen where he put on a pot of coffee and began frying some sausages, knowing that would bring her out.

Two minutes later, just as he assumed, she walked out into the kitchen. Cooper turned from the stove. "Hey, good morning."

She mumbled, "Good morning."

Peeking at the baby, who appeared to be over her virus and actually looked bubbly and perky, he said, "Wow, look at Daphne. She's back to normal."

Zoe said, "Yeah, she's great," but her response was so subdued, Cooper peered at her. Her cheeks were flushed. Her eyes were glassy. Oh, Lord! Unease squeezed his stomach. "You're not sick, are you?"

She didn't answer. Instead, she walked to the stove. "What are you making that smells so awful?"

"Sausage."

She gave him a dismayed look. "Oh, no!" she said, then shoved Daphne at him. "I think I have to throw up."

Cooper just barely caught the baby before Zoe raced away. Holding Daphne at arm's distance, he stared at her. She stared back. "This will only take a minute," he told the baby, hoping he was correct.

She let out a yowl.

Cooper said, "Right," then waited. And waited. And waited.

Finally, realizing something might really be wrong, he carried Daphne into the bedroom, around the bed and to the corner bathroom. "Everything okay in there?" he called.

Zoe opened the door and came out. "No. Everything is not okay. I'm really sick."

A ripple of dread swept over Cooper. "What, exactly, does 'really sick' mean?"

"It means you'll have to care for Daphne today…at least for a few hours. It was only a twenty-four-hour bug. I felt myself getting sick last night. I'll be better by this time tomorrow."

"This time tomorrow!" His eyes widened with horror. His stomach plummeted. "I can't care for Daphne!"

"You have to," she said, then fell to the bed facedown, as if she didn't have the energy to get into bed like a normal person.

"You don't understand. I *can't!* I don't know how."

"I thought you had all kinds of experience with baby cows."

"They don't wear diapers."

She didn't even lift her head. "I'm sorry, Bryant. But

you've got to do this. And you can. I didn't have anybody teach me how to care for her. My mother's in California, remember? I figured it all out myself. Except for special case scenarios like yesterday's virus, Daphne is actually fairly self-explanatory."

"You think she is, but…" He glanced at the bed. Zoe was out. He glanced at Daphne. She patted his cheek, then shifted her hand, grabbed at the stubble of whiskers on his chin and twisted.

"Ouch!"

Daphne laughed.

Cooper groaned. "Zoe?"

She didn't even move. Cooper almost fell to the bed in frustration. He did not know one thing about caring for a baby, but it looked as though he was about to learn.

Chapter Four

"Okay, how hard can this be?" Cooper said, using psychology on himself as he walked Daphne out to the kitchen again.

Hadn't he faced greater challenges?

Shoot, yes!

When he left Arkansas, he had about three hundred bucks. The only job experience he had was working for the family construction business with two brothers who didn't like him, so he couldn't name them on a résumé. Nonetheless, he found a company similar to the one he and his brothers had inherited when his parents had died, and he got a job as a laborer.

Because he really had been a construction worker and even had experience running the family company, he rose quickly through the ranks and not only saved lots of money, he also found a friend who wanted to be partners with him on a ranch. Once they bought the ranch,

he easily got his commercial driver's license—CDL—
and found a trucking company that would employ him
when he needed quick cash. The ranch couldn't be depended on to make money, let alone provide instant
funds when an unexpected bill came along. Driving
truck didn't require him to be on the job at 9:00 a.m.
every Monday and gave him long stretches of time off.
It was perfect.

The system worked so well Cooper drove truck a lot.
First, he did it to get the resources he and his partner
needed for improvements to the existing outbuildings on
the ranch. Then he began saving to increase the herd so
that he could finally retire from trucking and ranch full-
time. Instead, the cattle money was going to pay off the
mortgage, but that was okay, because it would only take
a few years driving truck to restore it again. And then
he really would be on his own. The ranch would be his.
The herd would be paid for. No bank…no *brother*
would have any claim on him.

When he wanted to be, Cooper knew he was re-
sourceful. And determined. And strong.

Surely to hell he could take care of one measly baby.

"Last night your mother opened some applesauce,"
he told Daphne, who screeched and slapped his cheek.
"That's what you're having for breakfast."

She hooked her fingers in his nose and twisted.

"Ouch! Geez, kid," he said, catching her chubby little hand and holding it so she couldn't grab anything
else on his face. "You could disfigure me at the rate
you're going."

She laughed.

Cooper sighed. "Right."

Luckily the baby seat was still in the kitchen. Cooper buckled Daphne in and then retrieved the applesauce. He remembered his discussion with Zoe about feeding Daphne. He also recalled watching her slide the spoon into the baby's mouth. He could do this.

He pulled a chair up to the table and popped the lid off the short, stout jar. He stuck the spoon into the ground apples, pulled out a healthy portion and aimed it for Daphne's mouth.

Her eyes widened and her lips parted. Clearly, she was hungry. That was good.

He slid the spoon along her tongue, being careful not to shove it in too far or too fast. Daphne gulped the food. Unfortunately, before she swallowed, she grinned at him and applesauce came pouring out of her mouth.

"Shoot!" Remembering what he'd seen Zoe do the night before, Cooper caught the wayward applesauce with the spoon before it dripped off Daphne's chin and onto her chest. Because if that happened he would have to change her shirt and he absolutely, positively was not doing that.

"Come on, kid. Work with me here."

She laughed and patted her hands on her thighs.

"Okay. No yelping. I'm giving you another spoon of this stuff, so you need to calm down."

Having learned his lesson, Cooper judiciously measured the second helping—careful not to give her so much the residual rolled out. He cautiously slid it into her mouth and when she grinned with joy there was no surplus to dribble out. Most of it stayed on the back of her tongue where he'd put it.

He damned near whooped with excitement over his

success. But not taking anything for granted, he didn't whoop until he fed her half the jar. After that she began to blow bubbles with it and Cooper had a theory. Anytime a woman started playing with her food, she was either on a diet, unhappy with the entrée or not really hungry. He chose number three and rose from his seat.

"Good job," he said, then winced when he realized that was exactly what he told his horse when they returned from mending fences. But, really, caring for Daphne was a lot like dealing with an animal. She couldn't speak. He was never really certain she understood what he said. And she didn't realize that things she thought were fun could wound him.

By the time he got the applesauce in the refrigerator, Daphne was no longer spitting or slapping her chubby palms on her equally chubby thighs. In fact, she appeared to be downright calm. So calm she looked to be in the mood for an after-breakfast nap.

Fine by him.

He opened the refrigerator again and took out the last of her bottles. That would have panicked him, but he had more important concerns. He wasn't entirely sure how this part went, but he suspected he couldn't simply hand her a bottle and tell her to go to sleep. In movies and on TV he had seen mothers feed bottles to babies while rocking them. Because that seemed like an excellent formula to get the kid back to sleep, he unbuckled her from her seat, plucked her out and headed for the rocker, bottle in hand.

With a sigh, and glad that absolutely none of his trucker co-workers could see him, he dropped to the rocker, arranged the kid across his lap, pillowed her head on his forearm and slid the bottle into her mouth. She began to suck. He began to rock. Too late, he realized he should have turned on the TV so he would have something to do while she drank her milk. But that ship had sailed. So he rocked back and forth, watching her suck down half the contents of her bottle and noticing that her eyelids quickly became droopy and began to drift shut.

He shook his head in amazement. This was so darned easy he really had to wonder why parents whined about caring for kids. When Daphne's eyes had been closed for about two minutes, Cooper knew he could lay her down. But, as he rose from the rocker, congratulating himself on the good mothering he had just done, he realized that Zoe was asleep in the room at the back of the hall. Not only was she sick, but she'd thrown herself sideways across the bed.

Well...okay. That ruled out Daphne's usual sleeping place. But no problem. He would take her upstairs.

He climbed the steps, intending to secure her on one of the two single beds in the room across from his, but they were too thin. If she rolled twice, she could fall off. So Daphne couldn't stay in the spare room.

He carried her into the bedroom he had been using, but he realized that though this bed was wider than the singles in the other room, it was too high. If she rolled off, she'd fall so far she'd probably be hurt.

So, the first bed was being wholly taken by her mother. The second beds were too thin. The third was too far off the ground. He sighed again. At some point even Goldilocks found a bed that was just right.

Daphne stirred in his arms with a whimper. He

quickly began to rock her back to sleep. "Shhhhh," he crooned, then rolled his eyes heavenward. He was so glad there wasn't anybody around to witness this!

But Daphne didn't quiet down from the rocking or the crooning. Instead, she stretched, her eyes opened, her face puckered and she began to cry.

"Oh, no! No. No. No. Come on, kid! Remember, I'm not a pro. I need some…"

He stopped talking, then sniffed the air. Dear God!

"Oh, Daphne! Darn it, kid! I hadn't yet worked my-self up to change a *wet* diaper. I can't handle what you cooked up down there!"

Daphne began to cry in earnest.

"Shhhhh," he soothed, then groaned when he got another whiff of what he knew was in her diaper. "Your mom owes me big-time," he said as he turned and jogged down the steps, holding Daphne about two feet away from himself.

Luckily he'd brought the diaper bag into the kitchen the night before. He grabbed it and pulled out a dispos-able diaper, but he suddenly realized there was nowhere to change her, so he turned and ran upstairs again, back to the room he was using with the bigger bed.

He laid her down and ripped open the front snaps of her one-piece pajamas. Not quite sure what to do then, he studied the situation and realized he would have to take her legs out of the pajamas to get her diaper off.

He did that. Then examined the diaper, noting the strips of tape on either side. With a resigned sigh, he yanked open both tape tabs and then groaned at what awaited him. Especially when he realized that he had left the diaper bag—and therefore the wet cloths—downstairs.

He didn't have any choice but to make the best of the situation and eventually got her cleaned up and a new diaper installed. By the time he slid her legs into the pajamas again, she was laughing.

"Oh, yeah, that was really funny."

She gooed delightedly.

He sighed and reminded himself he had not died. He had successfully completed the diaper change. And there was no point in being negative.

"All right. Let's go downstairs and find something on TV."

Daphne didn't argue, so Cooper grabbed her from the bed and jogged downstairs. He found the remote, turned on the television and settled on watching a rerun of a docudrama. Unfortunately, he couldn't lie on the couch with Daphne. That meant he was back to the rocker. But Daphne wasn't happy. She squiggled and squirmed as if she wanted to get down. And Cooper supposed she could. The great room was huge and there weren't a lot of things she could bump into if she rolled. The only problem was that he couldn't be sure it was clean.

So he jogged up the stairs again, Daphne on his arm, yanked the spread from his bed, and carried it to the great room. One-handed, he managed to open it on the floor. Then he placed Daphne in its center. On a stroke of genius, he ran to her diaper bag and found a few toys. He tossed them to the blanket beside her. She looked up at him and grinned.

He grinned back. Success again. He was no longer so cocky that he would criticize any parent. But he had figured out some fairly sticky problems. He knew he wasn't perfect but he thought he was pretty darned good at this.

Ultimately, Daphne played herself out. Without a word or help from Cooper, who had decided to watch television from a prone position on the sofa, she laid her head on the bedspread, made herself comfortable and fell asleep. Also played out from his morning, Cooper fell asleep, too.

Ten minutes later he heard a scream and launched off the couch as if someone had set off a starting gun. He immediately looked at the blanket where he'd left Daphne and much to his horror she was gone.

Luckily, she screamed again. Cooper pivoted in the direction of the noise.

"Oh, my God! Daphne!" he yelped, scrambling over to the section of the room from which her cries and frustrated screams and screeches were coming. She'd somehow gotten wedged between the television stand and a bookcase.

He caught her up in his arms. "How the heck did you do that?"

She sniffled and looked away.

"All right. It's probably a trade secret. I can respect that. Want some more milk?"

He figured that if he fed her more of her bottle she would take another nap. He wasn't sure how she had gotten herself wedged so far away from where he put her, but this time he simply wouldn't go to sleep. He would watch TV with one eye on her in case she decided to roll again.

She drank the remainder of the last bottle, dozed off, and continued sleeping when he laid her in the center of the blanket on the floor again. He sighed with relief and went back to his television show. But what seemed like only a few seconds later she was crying. This time he found her wedged between the two chairs.

He picked her up again. "Okay. Two times means you haven't learned some kind of lesson yet. I don't even know how you're getting where you're going, but I'm hoping being trapped twice taught you your lesson."

He sat her down on the blanket. She grabbed for a rattle. Cooper went back to TV.

This time when she howled, he found her on all fours backed into a corner and he suddenly saw what she was doing. "You can only crawl backward!"

She made a grunting noise while rocking on her knees as if trying to push through the wall behind her.

"You've got to come forward, kid."

She screeched with unhappiness.

Cooper stooped down and moved her right arm forward. "This way." He thought she would mimic the movement with her other arm and go forward. Instead she simply slid the arm he had moved back to its original position.

Given that she didn't appear to be a quick learner and he wasn't anybody's teacher, he scooped her from the floor again. Unfortunately, he caught the aroma of something he didn't like and he groaned. "Not again!"

She laughed.

In the bedroom he was using, he repeated the diaper ritual, but this time with all the necessary equipment. Clean and happy, Daphne again settled on the blanket to play, but she never did nap.

By the time evening rolled around, Cooper was exhausted and Daphne wasn't much better. She could play on the floor, but she couldn't sleep on the floor because the second she awakened, she crawled backward into some kind of trouble. But the bed situation on the second floor hadn't changed and Daphne's mother was still using the downstairs bed. Zoe had only come out once to check on things, but she'd been so weak and feverish she'd damned near fainted so Cooper had shooed her back to bed.

Worse, Daphne had drunk the remainder of the last bottle. There were empties on the counter by the sink, but there was no milk to fill them. The only thing Cooper could give her was water and that earned him a bop with the same bottle he had filled for her.

As nine o'clock quickly approached, Cooper rocked a very cranky baby with no idea where he'd put her down for the night and absolutely positive he couldn't hold her for one more second.

"All right," he told sobbing Daphne. "I can't do anything about the milk, but we're going on a quest for a bed for you. And this time, we're thinking outside the box."

He carried the baby upstairs again, not even glancing at the single beds or the bed he had been using because he already knew they were worthless. He scanned the room, reminding himself to think creatively, and then he saw a wicker laundry basket.

Small, but somewhat tall, the basket had the look of a crib or cradle of sorts. He slid it out of the corner, positive he could put in on the floor beside his bed and hear Daphne if she awakened. It seemed perfect. But by the time he lined it with a blanket there wasn't any room left for Daphne.

He glanced around the room again. With the wicker basket and the bed out of play, the only thing left in the room was a mirrored dresser. He frowned at it. He remembered reading a story in grade school about a poor family who had been forced to have their baby sleep in a dresser drawer.

He pulled one of the drawers from the empty dresser. It wasn't quite as tall as the basket, but it was much wider and longer. There was plenty of room for Daphne *and* a blanket. He lined it with a quiltlike blanket that acted as a makeshift mattress, laid her inside and gave her the bottle of water.

Sitting on the edge of his bed, he watched her drink enough to settle herself and ultimately fall asleep. Then he took the bottle and set it on the dresser, turned out the light and collapsed on the bed.

When Daphne woke at two, Cooper knew she wasn't going to let him get back to sleep. After no nap the day before, she had been too tired to protest the water, but with five hours of sleep behind her she wouldn't settle for second best. His only hope was to rock her until she drifted off but he had a sneaking suspicion that wasn't going to work.

He took the dresser drawer downstairs, settled Daphne inside and turned on the TV.

Zoe awakened the next morning feeling a bit stiff and sore, but no longer weak and dizzy. She rolled out of bed, tested her health by standing without holding onto anything and pronounced herself well. Then she remembered she'd abdicated Daphne's care to a perfect stranger and ran out of the bedroom.

In the great room, she skidded to a stop and her eyes widened at the scene that greeted her. A comforter had been spread across the center of the floor. On top of the comforter was a dresser drawer lined with a blanket. On top of the blanket was her sleeping baby. And atop her sleeping baby was the long arm of the rancher/trucker who was lying on the floor beside her.

Zoe couldn't tell if he was keeping an arm across Daphne as a sort of early warning system for when she awoke, or if it was a sign of affection. She only knew the scene was adorable.

She sat on the sofa, staring at sleeping Cooper Bryant. He was without a doubt the most complicated man she had ever met. He liked to be alone, yet he was too good to ignore her and too kindhearted to desert Daphne when she needed him. But, kind as he was, he didn't get along with his own brothers. It didn't make any sense.

Unless his brothers were real losers.

She took a deep breath, deciding that would be more acceptable if Cooper were married, proving there was at least somebody he got along with. Or maybe if he had a different job. Truckers were loners. Ranchers could be loners. Loners were usually difficult people.

Still, Cooper had said he had a partner. And he and his partner had a mortgage, which Cooper's brothers had bought in order to take his ranch away from him. And what else had he said? They already had his family inheritance. They got it by default when he left them.

Looking at Cooper, sleeping on the floor, one arm laid protectively across her baby, it appeared the whole fault of Cooper's troubles belonged with his brothers.

Except Cooper wasn't exactly Mr. Personality, and he could have driven his brothers to the point where they might have felt justified to ask him to leave.

Rising from the sofa and heading for the kitchen, she cursed under her breath. Damn it! Why was she so curious about him? Because he was so good-looking?

The question made her stop. She turned around to study him again. She studied his soft-looking black hair, the smooth lines of his handsome face, the solid build of his shoulders and back and his cute butt, and she sighed. His good looks should have turned her off. That was the rule she'd made when Brad had left. No more good-looking men. And she'd stuck to it, too. So, she wasn't continually thinking about Cooper Bryant because of his good looks. She also didn't feel sorry for him. She continued to be curious about him because of the way he treated *her*.

Chauvinist that he was, he nonetheless recognized her strength, but he didn't assume that because she was strong he could ignore her. They were sharing a house, so they really did "share." He hadn't fended for himself for breakfast, lunch and dinner. They had eaten together. When Daphne had been sick, and Zoe had sat on the bedroom floor watching over her, he might not have known how to make her child better, but he'd wanted to do something. She could see his desire to help in his expressions and in the way he couldn't simply ignore her.

In fact, having him stay and talk with her while Daphne slept had been odd for *her* to accept. She hadn't chosen to be a loner. She certainly didn't like being a loner. But she was. Just as Cooper's brothers had gotten his family inheritance by default, she had become a loner by default. She wasn't someone anybody catered to. She was someone people typically left alone. Hell, she was someone people *pushed* away!

"Be who you want to be," her mother had said, right before she'd hugged her only child and taken off in her SUV for California.

Her father had said, "In this world you have to be strong, princess, and I'm glad you are." Then he'd slammed the door on his U-Haul and twenty seconds later she was watching him drive out of her life.

"Pregnant?" her husband had said before he'd basically fallen to their sofa, staring at her as if he were trying to comprehend the word.

But as quickly as he'd fallen in disbelief, he'd risen. "You know what? You can handle this, babe, but I can't." He walked into their bedroom and, as if it were the logical thing to do, just started packing. "You're strong," he'd said. "But *I* can't do this."

He'd said a few other things, then he was gone, too. She'd tried to talk him out of it, of course. She'd scrambled after him as he'd strode to his car, giving him assurances that he could handle being a dad, but he'd kept shaking his head, arguing that he couldn't.

She'd hoped that after a day or two away, he would miss her. But he hadn't. And that had upset her more than his not wanting their baby because she knew that was the bottom line. If he had loved her, a pregnancy wouldn't have scared him off. But he hadn't loved her.

So he'd told her she was strong and left her.

Cooper Bryant was the first person who recognized her strength, accepted it and yet still stayed.

True, they were stranded together because two feet

of snow had fallen on the mountain, and he couldn't leave. She frowned. He might be trapped with her, but he didn't have to talk to her and that was the point. Cooper could be ignoring her. Yet he wasn't. And since he wasn't a naturally nice person, the only explanation could be that he liked her.

She blinked. He liked her? Or he wanted to sleep with her?

He wanted to sleep with her. He'd already said it. Still, a man who wanted to sleep with her could ignore her child. Cooper Bryant had cared for Daphne.

In the kitchen, Zoe put coffee grounds into a filter and poured water into the reservoir of the coffeemaker, then tried to look out the window above the sink, but couldn't. Snow had crammed into the little squares of the screen, which the cabin owner hadn't removed from the summer, even though an entire fall had passed and winter had begun. They were now ten days away from Christmas. The holiday she had loved the most as a child. The holiday she missed the most as an adult. But at least now that she had Daphne she had a reason to put up a tree and buy presents.

The thought lifted her spirits. She didn't have a lot to spend on a celebration, but it didn't always take money to make a holiday happy. Not when there was a baby involved!

As the coffee dripped into the pot, she walked through the great room to the glass doors by the poker table and glanced out. There was definitely two feet of snow, but the sun was shining. The wind wasn't blowing. With Cooper and Daphne sleeping so soundly on the floor beside the TV, she couldn't turn it on to watch the Weather Channel, but she almost didn't have to. It wasn't snowing. The storm was over. They would be leaving today. The smart thing to do would be to shower and begin gathering her things while Daphne and her knight in shining armor slept.

When she reached the end of the great room and was about to enter the hall to her bedroom, she turned and looked at Cooper Bryant one more time. She wondered what his Christmas would be like. His parents had died and he was estranged from his brothers so she knew he didn't have a family tradition to attend. Did he celebrate with his partner? Did he celebrate at all? The thought that he would be as alone as she had been last Christmas squeezed her heart. With her husband gone, celebrating with the new woman in his life, and her parents both forgetting to phone, Zoe had experienced the worst day of her life. She could not imagine anybody would be that alone deliberately.

Would it be totally and completely inappropriate to invite him to her house for Christmas? She frowned, considering that. He lived in Texas. She lived in the mountains of Pennsylvania. It wasn't as if he could drive over the river and through the woods to get to her house.

Except…

She owed him. He had taken care of Daphne when she couldn't. And she still believed he needed somebody to talk to about his family. And she intended to have the best Christmas ever. Wouldn't it be nice to share that with him?

Of course it would. And if he was as alone as she believed he was, he might be willing to drive to Pennsylvania to avoid that long, lonely day. Heck, if he drove to Pennsylvania from Texas and then back again, even if he only spent one afternoon with her and Daphne, he could avoid the whole long, lonely holiday season!

Giving him the chance to sidestep that misery was the least she could do for the kindness he'd shown her.

Still, she didn't want to be pushy. Or invade his privacy.

But if he gave her one sign, one real, solid sign that he didn't want to be alone for Christmas, she would ask him.

But it had to be his decision. *He* had to give her a sign.

Chapter Five

Cooper awakened to the scent of fresh coffee. Disoriented, he sat up. His back was so stiff with prickly pain that he wondered if he'd slept on a bed of nails, then he glanced around and almost groaned. He was still in the god-awful house in the woods he'd found to shelter Zoe, her baby and himself. He was on the floor, sleeping atop the comforter that he'd originally spread out for Daphne, but which had become the only place he could sleep while still keeping an eye on her. It was no damned wonder his back ached. Then Daphne slapped him across the nose with her empty bottle.

"Don't try to make up with me now."

Daphne screeched joyfully.

"Oh, you're up."

At the sound of Zoe's voice, Cooper twisted to face the sofa, where she sat brushing her hair. Damp blond curls fell loosely past her shoulders. Her face had a freshly scrubbed look.

His first thought was that even right from a shower—with no makeup and wet hair—she was absolutely gorgeous. His second thought was that she was "up." Not just awake but full of energy.

"Daphne and I have already showered." She smiled prettily. "I like the drawer idea, by the way. That's why I put her back in after I cleaned her up. She can't really crawl, except backwards and she gets herself in all kinds of trouble. Putting her in the drawer is a nice way to keep her in the room with us without having to watch her every move."

Relief poured through Cooper. He was so damn glad she wasn't sick that he forgot his back hurt. He forgot the long night with the baby, who screamed nonstop because the only thing he could put in her bottle was water. He forgot he'd had fewer than two hours of actual sleep. All he could focus on was how damned wonderful Zoe looked. Awake! Alert! Not sick!

"I made coffee," she said, rising from the couch and casually padding in her sock-covered feet to the kitchen, where she extracted two mugs from the dish drainer beside the sink.

He scrambled off the floor and nearly ran to the kitchen.

Facing the coffeepot, she couldn't see that he had followed her and she called, "Would you like me to bring a cup into the great room for you?"

She should throw him a damned parade. She should pay for an X-ray of his face to see if her daughter's head butting, bottle slapping and skin grabbing had caused any real damage.

Holding two mugs of steaming coffee, she turned but stopped short when she saw he was right behind her. She smiled. "Are you that desperate for coffee?"

"I'm that desperate for help with your child." He took both mugs from her hands and set them on the counter before he clasped her shoulders and stared into her eyes. "You're really well?"

She laughed. "I feel terrific. Sorry about yesterday. I—"

She didn't get to finish her sentence because Cooper kissed her. He had never been so happy to see anyone well as he was to see Zoe up and about and capable of caring for her own baby. And he wanted to thank her simply for being alive, but when his lips pressed to hers, an odd thing happened. The absolute softness of her mouth caused him to forget all about appreciation and to head directly to the sexual place he'd been telling himself was off-limits unless Zoe gave him the go-ahead.

Falling headfirst into wonderland, his thoughts rolled to things like satin sheets, perfumed oils, bubble bath and wine, as his body tensed with anticipation. He deepened the kiss and let ripple upon ripple of pleasure pour through him.

Just as he was about to declare kissing her the definition of heaven, he realized he was *kissing* her. Not thanking her. Not kissing her for joy. But honest-to-God kissing her as if they were about to tumble into bed.

He jerked away, but that did nothing to lessen the flood of hormones replacing the blood in his arteries and veins. Dear God. Kissing her wasn't merely powerful. It was potent. She was soft. She smelled good. She fit against him. And everything in his body responded to that quickly, easily, naturally. Almost as if he didn't have any control.

But he did have control. He *always* had control.

His gaze jumped to catch hers and what he saw in her eyes shot conflicting reactions through him. She was not confused. She liked the kiss. If the gooey expression on her face was anything to go by, she liked *him*. If he kissed her again, as his hormones were voting he do, she wouldn't stop him. She might even let him take her to bed.

Though his body tensed and tightened and damned near took over for his mind, he managed to find a few functioning brain cells and focused on the other side of this deal. He might have been trying to get her into bed for the past two days, but he'd never expected her to take him up on it. The very fact that she "liked" him made him realize he couldn't take them down that road. She was not the kind of woman a man trifled with. She was the kind of woman a man settled down with. And Cooper was not the settling down kind. Hell, women should thank him for realizing that about himself and staying away from them.

But he didn't think Zoe was going to thank him. She had too many stars in her eyes.

Shoot!

He pulled his hands from her shoulders and stepped away. "Okay, that was supposed to be a gee-I'm-glad-you're-better kiss. I'm sorry it got out of hand."

She stared at him for a few seconds as if she couldn't respond. Well, he certainly understood that. That kiss had rolled through him like a thunderstorm in Oklahoma. It was a miracle he could talk. It was a miracle he could think. But he had thought. Thank God. And because he had enough presence of mind to realize kissing the way they had been was wrong, he was getting them out of this before the ideas clearly rumbling through Zoe's brain went too far.

He grabbed his mug of coffee, downed it and turned toward the front door. "I have a change of clothes in my truck." He set the mug on the countertop. Zoe continued to stare at him. "A shower sounds like heaven now, but a change of clothes sounds better. Plus, I think it's time I checked on road conditions. The snow has stopped, but that doesn't mean the roads have been cleared."

Zoe found her voice. "You have a radio."

She said it as a fact, not a question, but he nodded anyway. "Yeah."

He didn't give her any more answer than that, and went in search of his boots. Once he had them on, he didn't reiterate his mission or even say goodbye. He simply headed for the door. Shoving his hands into the pockets of his lined denim jacket, he trudged through the two feet of snow to the driveway. Because it was dark when they'd arrived, he and Zoe hadn't seen the easier access to the house and had bounded up the front yard. In the daytime he not only saw the driveway and garage, he saw the path to the road.

Focused on getting to his truck, he refused to let himself think of anything but trekking through the snow. When he reached the road, he groaned. Sparkling with reflected sunlight, the white blanket on the highway and in the surrounding woods hadn't been touched by man or vehicle. No one had walked or driven on this road since the storm had started Friday night.

With a resigned breath, Cooper made the first line of footprints in the perfect snow. He would have thought it a shame to ruin something so beautiful since it was clear no one was leaving that day, but he had to get the hell away from Zoe.

Though he hadn't let himself venture anywhere near thoughts of Zoe, the kiss, her reaction, or even his reaction while he'd walked down the driveway, his subconscious hadn't let any of it go. Like a dog with a bone it gnawed at his brain, reminding him he was in trouble.

Zoe liked him. Maybe because he'd cared for her daughter, maybe because she was a dreamer, or maybe because of a combination of the two, she had gotten the mistaken impression that he was someone worth liking. But he knew he wasn't. Given half a chance, he would take advantage of her naive assumptions about him. If he played his cards right, spoke nicely, pretended to be the person she thought, she would let her guard down that night. He could make love to her for the rest of their stay and be gone two seconds after the snowplow went through—without a backward glance.

But she deserved better than that.

He pulled his Stetson down to block the blinding glare of the sun off the wind-packed snow. Of course, if he had misjudged her and she wasn't looking for a permanent relationship, he might be rejecting something really, really good.

Cooper kicked the snow. Hard. That was genuine wishful thinking. It was as ridiculous for him to even consider she wanted a one-night stand as it was for her to think he was some kind of knight in shining armor.

He trudged up the hill, gratefully unlocked the truck

door and climbed into the cab. He nearly hugged the steering wheel because, to him, this vehicle meant freedom. Lots of days he was secretly glad he could get away from everything, head for the open road and just listen to country music stations from Texas to Canada. Having this job prevented arguments with his partner, saved him and his partner from growing tired of each other's company, gave his partner a chance to bring women to the ranch and gave Cooper a chance to find women in unexpected places.

And kept him from being with any one person so long that she got all the wrong ideas.

When Bonnie—a seemingly easygoing, undemanding woman he dated and might have actually considered settling down with—had dumped him five years ago, she'd said he all but ignored her and he knew it was true. He had thought she was the kind of woman who didn't care about all the touchy-feely stuff other women wanted. But, apparently she had. And he had missed the signals she had been tossing out for him to understand that. Most days he didn't think of anything but the obvious, which for him always had something to do with his own personal well-being. That was actually why he'd cared for Daphne. Not because he was *nice* but because it was common sense. If he didn't feed her and entertain her she would scream. He hated screaming. So he'd cared for the baby to make his own life more comfortable.

But how did a guy explain that to a woman with stars in her eyes?

He didn't.

He should leave. Right now. He was out the door. There hadn't been a scene. He hadn't made a promise he wouldn't keep. He hadn't even led Zoe on. She might be dreamy-eyed about the kiss and think about him for an hour or so. She might even sputter and spit a bit when she realized he wasn't coming back. But he wouldn't have hurt her. She'd forget him within a day or two of getting home.

Unfortunately, he could not get his truck up this mountain when there was at least two feet of snow on the road. He might be able to get down....

Damn! He knew that was too dangerous. Besides, it wouldn't be fair to Zoe simply to leave.

Yet, it also wouldn't be fair to Zoe to go back to that house with her having the wrong idea about that kiss.

On the other hand, if he didn't go back, she might not curse him and sputter about irresponsible men. She could worry that he had been hurt. And that wasn't fair. Worse, if he didn't go back and the furnace broke, she and Daphne might freeze. The kid was already out of milk. Water had kept her from killing him the night before, but if this road didn't get plowed in the next few days...

He sighed. When in the hell had his life gotten so complicated?

Friday afternoon. When his semi had lost its ability to go forward.

With another sigh, he raised a trucker on his radio and asked about road conditions. Things were bad. Twenty-four to thirty-six inches of snow had fallen. The state had begun to plow, but even the main arteries weren't open yet.

Cooper thanked the trucker and wished him well, then signed off and did what he knew he had to do. He pulled a duffel bag of spare clothes from the compartment behind his seat and tossed it in the space beside him, ready to take it with him when he went back to the house because he knew his conscience wouldn't let him leave Zoe and Daphne alone. Plus, now that the storm itself had subsided, he had to get his check. Nobody would be driving up the mountain, but anybody walking by could break into his truck and steal the one and only true valuable he had.

He leaned around and removed the cover that hid the safe, then fiddled with the lock. When it opened, he pulled out the white envelope containing the certified check. He wished he hadn't been forced to pay off the mortgage now, but he had no choice.

Just as he had no choice but to go back to that house. He couldn't strand Zoe. So he was stuck. And his libido was just going to have to play gin rummy or something until he could leave. He was sure the road would be cleared in another day or two. Forty-eight hours wasn't that long to control himself. Lord knows, he'd done it before.

That logic satisfied him until he returned to the house. Zoe stood in the hallway that separated the open great room from the kitchen. Her pretty yellow hair had dried and hung sexily around her, but her blue eyes were wide and round as if she hadn't expected him to return.

But as if she realized he really was standing in the foyer, she hadn't conjured him in her imagination, her entire face changed, relaxed, became filled with relief. And Cooper felt something inside him respond to that look. He didn't feel happy. He didn't feel glad to be back. What he felt was something more primal, more instinctive. It was almost a sense of duty that had clicked in. As if he had a mate's responsibility to this woman. Worse, that feeling of responsibility didn't fill him with fear or anger. It felt very natural.

That almost made him groan. First, he could not be responsible for someone he didn't really know. Second, he never put his name and the word "mate" in the same thought process with a woman. Something was terribly wrong here and he suddenly suspected he knew what it was. Because he'd cared for Daphne, his desire to seduce Zoe had come head-to-head with her motherhood. So to make seducing her acceptable, he was thinking like a mate. Not a husband…God forbid. But something more primitive. Because he wanted to be primitive with her. The way he wanted to make love to her was raw and natural, not nice or respectable.

The very fact that he couldn't stop thinking about this should have scared him silly but he capped the hypothesis by realizing that by respecting Zoe, he was actually giving her the wrong idea. When he thought that he knew he'd finally gotten to the bottom line. Unless he wanted her hearts-and-flowers notions to take root, he had to stop being nice to her.

The easy way for him to get her to dislike and mistrust him the way she had originally would be to make a pass at her. Not implement some sweet seduction, but make a cool, calculated suggestion, as he had when he'd been willing to trade his story for sex. If he came on to her as his true I-only-want-sex self, their relationship would probably go back to normal. No thoughts of kisses or "having feelings."

Yeah, he was going back to behaving like his obnoxious self. No more of this letting her think he was Mr. Nice Guy.

He wasn't.

For Zoe, the rest of the morning and afternoon passed almost like a typical day at home. She made a fresh batch of formula, earning a groan from Cooper, who had apparently endured Daphne's temper the night before because he hadn't had anything but water to put in her bottle.

Then she found a washing machine in the basement, and though she had to hang her and Daphne's clothes on a line she strung in the great room, by the end of the afternoon they had something clean to wear.

Cooper watched replays of classic games on a sports channel and only grunted when she tried to make conversation. At first she thought he might be angry that he had been forced to care for Daphne the day before, but then she remembered the real reason he'd left her alone that morning. His thank-you kiss had turned into something he hadn't intended it to be. And his response wasn't the only unexpected reaction. She could all too easily recall the softness of his lips, the way he nibbled and nipped and finally given himself over to the incredible kiss. And when he'd fallen over the edge, she had, too. How could she help it? The man dripped sex appeal. He was gorgeous, street-smart, worldly. If she hadn't known that before he kissed her, she certainly knew it now.

Peeling potatoes to put around the roast she had baking, Zoe suppressed a shiver. No first kiss had ever stolen her breath the way his had. No kiss had ever reached into her soul with emotion the way his had. But Cooper Bryant was nothing like the man she envisioned herself with in her second time around romantically. She didn't want somebody so practiced in the ways of the world. She wanted an average guy. She didn't want someone brimming with sex appeal. She wanted a guy who wanted a family.

And Cooper had abandoned his family.

She stopped her thoughts and took another breath. He'd said his brothers had kicked him out of their lives, but it was fairly clear from the things he said and how he behaved that he kept himself out. He absolutely, positively, definitely was the wrong, wrong, wrong guy for her.

However...

She had asked for a sign that he might want an invitation to Christmas dinner and if that kiss wasn't a sign, she didn't know what was.

More than that, though, she didn't know everything about him. Heck, she hardly knew *anything* about him. There could be extenuating circumstances in his family situation. He might secretly long for everything she wanted and simply be unable to admit it because he was still hurting from his brothers' rejection....

Boy, was she ever reaching! Particularly since his behavior after the kiss had negated any sort of message she'd thought was in that kiss. He'd grabbed the first excuse to leave the house, and when he'd returned he hadn't spoken one word beyond his groanings about Daphne's formula. Not even to tell her about the road conditions. She'd assumed he hadn't heard anything good since he'd brought his duffel bag, showered and changed into clean clothes before settling on the sofa. So she hadn't asked and he hadn't volunteered.

He was clearly sorry he'd kissed her. But that was fine since he wasn't right for her. He was too old, too complicated. The last thing either one of them needed was to get involved with the other.

The best thing to do would be forget that kiss happened. And she would. Because that was the right thing to do. For both of them.

With the potatoes in the oven, she strolled into the great room again. Casually. Confidently. The same way she had Saturday morning before either one of them had even considered kissing. Positive this behavior would take them back to how they'd felt about each other before that kiss.

"You never told me if you raised anyone on your radio."

"I did."

She smiled. And he was right back to being as rude as he had been on Saturday morning. Thank God. "And what did this person say?"

"About what?"

"About the road conditions. Did you get any information?"

"Parts of the valley actually got thirty-six inches of snow."

She gasped.

"My thought exactly." He nestled into the sofa, as if to get back to his classic game. "So even the main arteries aren't open. My guess is we have another two days before anyone remembers there's a road on this mountain."

"Oh my God!"

"I couldn't have said it better myself."

He shifted his gaze to the television and Zoe knew the conversation was over. Fine. She'd endured a weekend of him already. She could do another two days.

She checked on Daphne, who continued to sleep soundly in the drawer on the floor of the bedroom, but when she walked into the hall again she realized she had absolutely nothing to do. Except straighten the kitchen. Though they continually tidied up their messes, it wouldn't hurt her to do a little extra cleaning. Maybe dust out a cupboard. Wipe down the refrigerator.

Because the owner of the house was a basically neat person—or family—arranging the cupboards and wiping out the refrigerator took only an hour. When Zoe was done, she paced behind the sofa so Cooper couldn't see her, but she was beginning to get annoyed with the way he hogged the television. She understood that he was angry with himself for kissing her, probably angry with himself for being nice to her, and even angry with himself for insisting she come along with him Friday afternoon to find shelter, but that didn't give him the right to make her miserable.

Luckily before she could say anything to him Daphne woke. Without taking her from the bedroom, Zoe changed her and played with her. When the timer on the stove rang, she came out, turned off the oven, fed Daphne some baby food, then served dinner for herself and Cooper. But rather than eat at the table, he fixed himself a plate and took it into the great room where he continued to watch TV. With Daphne in her travel seat, Zoe cleaned the kitchen. When that was done, she bathed the baby, put her in fresh pajamas, fed her a bottle and put her to sleep.

She almost lay down on her bed too, but she wasn't tired. And, damn it, she was bored and that stupid Cooper had hogged the one and only form of entertainment long enough.

She stormed into the great room. "Give me the remote!"

Drowsy, Cooper raised his gaze to meet Zoe's. He knew she was bored. He'd deliberately squandered the television. He'd not spoken. He'd eaten alone. All so she would realize he was an inconsiderate, selfish guy who wasn't going to change.

If he kissed her now, she'd probably slap his face.

He sat up on the sofa. "Sorry," he said a tad arrogantly, as if he were clueless to the fact that he'd been rude. He tossed the remote at her, then patted the sofa cushion beside him.

Looking as if she hadn't expected his easy acquiescence, Zoe cautiously caught the remote and even more cautiously sat. She hit a few buttons, bypassing the nightly news, two sitcoms and a movie in favor of an hour-long drama that she probably suspected they both would enjoy.

Even when she was mad at him she couldn't help being nice.

She was such a babe in the woods that Cooper almost felt guilty for what he was about to do, but not quite. He wanted to kill her infatuation. He didn't want her thinking he was something he wasn't. He didn't want her sympathy. He didn't want her affection. If she could make love without any of those, then he was her guy. If not, he wanted that out in the open, too, so she didn't accidentally tiptoe back to her crazy ideas about him.

As she became engrossed in the television show, he slowly raised his arm along the back of the sofa, resting it behind her. She appeared not to notice.

He inched closer. This time she shifted uneasily and glanced at him in her peripheral vision. Jerking his eyes in the direction of the television, he pretended not to see her looking at him. When she returned her attention to the show, he lifted his hand from the sofa back and gently dropped it on her shoulder.

For that she turned and stared at him. He frowned as if someone in the television show had done something confusing. When she glanced away, it was all he could do to hold back a smile. He'd never known that slowly making a pass at someone could be so amusing.

A commercial came on and neither one of them moved. He feigned being hypnotized by the screen. Zoe seemed as if she wasn't even breathing. When the show finally returned, and she relaxed enough to pay attention to the TV again, Cooper began playing with her hair.

Wow. Soft. And wonderfully springy. He glided his fingers through a curl and when he let it go, it rolled back. That made him smile. In fact, it completely stole his focus. This time when he slid his fingers through a thick lock, he watched them ripple through the strands, then watched her hair spring back into place.

"Your hair is amazing."

Cautious, she peeked at him. "It's naturally curly."

"Mine's straight," he said, then unwound a long lock to see it bounce back.

"Good for you."

He heard the slight quiver in her voice and realized

that while he had become analytical, she was falling victim to the movement of his hand through her hair. The knowledge that she was responding sent a shiver of arousal through him and reminded him to get back to his mission. This seduction wasn't supposed to be successful. He was supposed to disgust her. He shifted another few inches closer, let his hand drift from her hair to her shoulder and down her arm.

"What are you doing?"

He should have known that a talker like her wouldn't just get angry and tell him to stop. Nope. She wanted a syllabus.

"I'm seducing you. Should I give you the steps or is the broad definition enough?"

She stared at him. "Are you—"

Nuts? he suspected she was about to ask, so he kissed her before she could say anything else.

Her lips were as soft as he remembered, her mouth as yielding. Once again, Cooper felt himself tumble to the edge of reason, but this time he didn't let himself plummet over the precipice. He could enjoy a kiss, be drawn into a kiss, nibble and suckle and twine his tongue with her in a kiss, but he absolutely refused to lose control.

That was his last coherent thought before reason totally deserted him. Overwhelmed by her softness and the sheer pleasure of kissing her, he couldn't think of anything else, until suddenly, she jerked away from him and jumped off the sofa.

"You're *not* seducing me!"

"Why? Because I ignored you this afternoon? Honey, what's going on between you and me has nothing to do with getting along, or making a commitment or even exchanging phone numbers. And right now your body's telling me you feel the same things I do. Do you want to do this or not?"

"You are so crude!"

"I'm certainly not hearts and flowers." There. It was out. The thing he'd wanted to deny all day. The thing he wanted her to understand. The thing he needed for both of them to get beyond, so they could make these next two days at least passable.

"Well, I'm a hearts and flowers kind of girl."

"Hey, I didn't say I wouldn't be romantic."

"I don't want romance. I want love."

With that, she turned and left the room. Cooper heard her door slam and he reached for the remote, satisfied that any romantic notions she'd entertained had been killed.

But halfway to changing the channel, he realized he felt like scum. He tamped down the guilt by reminding himself that the air had needed clearing between them. But then he heard an odd sound. A click.

He rose from the sofa to see if he could determine the sound's origin and realized it had come from Zoe's bedroom. Specifically her bedroom door. He heard the click again. It was a key. Because the house was old, the bedrooms needed keys to lock them. Cooper hadn't thought to look for his, but apparently Zoe had found hers.

And she'd locked her door.

A foreign sensation gripped him. He felt creepy. She'd just told him she didn't trust him.

And she shouldn't. Her not trusting him shouldn't

bother him. He'd set out to make sure she knew what kind of man he was and clearly she now understood.

So why the hell did he care? And why the hell wouldn't this feeling of being a slime go away?

Chapter Six

Zoe stiffened when Cooper walked into the kitchen the following morning. Still fuming over his attempted seduction, she had spent the past hour tiptoeing around him while he had done exactly as he'd pleased, as if he didn't have a worry in the world.

She frowned. Damn it, he'd done that on purpose! He hadn't wanted to sleep with her the night before. He'd made the blatant pass at her to make a hundred percent sure she mistrusted him, as she had in the beginning, before his caring for Daphne had proved he wasn't such a bad guy. And before he'd kissed her in a way that made her toes curl.

He wanted her to remember he wasn't the kind of guy she could put any kind of faith in, so he'd simply reverted to the plan he'd been using all along to get her to keep her distance. After he'd behaved like an inconsiderate lout all day, he'd reminded her that the only thing he really wanted from her was a little physical fun.

And just as he'd expected, she'd run.

It made her so mad she longed to pop him. But she wouldn't. She was a nice girl.

And he counted on that, too.

He walked to the cabinet beside the sink, and Zoe fought the urge to inhale the fresh scent of his after-shave, then cursed herself for being attracted to such a hardheaded, argumentative pain in the butt. She couldn't understand why her hormones weren't getting the message that she shouldn't be interested in him, but they weren't. Anytime he got close to her, as he was now, a yearning billowed through her. Still, he was so gosh darn good looking, any woman would be attracted to him. Plus, he was experienced, funny and sexy. Physically perfect.

Listing his good qualities actually brought Zoe back to planet Earth and she shifted away from him. Dressed as she was, she felt like a dirt ball. Though she'd washed her clothes the day before, yesterday afternoon Daphne had spit baby food all over her. She was rumpled and grimy. He was clean, organized, in control. Even if she decided to break her rule not to get involved with another overly good-looking man, this particular hottie was way out of her league.

Of course, they weren't really on a level playing field. She had exactly two outfits she was rotating. As a trucker, he was accustomed to living out of a duffel bag. She wasn't even sure he had a house. On the other hand, she had a house, but it was partially empty because of her parents' scavenging when they'd moved.

Worse, her house was on the verge of being taken away. Her parents hadn't paid the taxes for years, and neither had thought to tell her that a few years ago when the amount was small enough she might have managed to squeeze it out of her own budget. But several years worth was too much for her to pay. This time next year *she* could be living out of a duffel bag.

Maybe she and Cooper weren't so different after all?

Without a word, Cooper grabbed a mug and poured himself a cup of coffee. Surreptitiously, Zoe watched him spoon in nondairy creamer. He wouldn't say good morning. He probably didn't feel he had to. He had made his wishes clear the night before. They were two ships passing in the night. If he wanted anything from her it was sex. If she wanted anything from him the price was sex. His life boiled down to basic needs, as if he intended to walk through without making a footprint. The way he lived allowed him to be in control and relatively content. And she couldn't help wondering if his philosophy wasn't right. After all, wanting more than just the basics only seemed to leave her wanting.

He made a sandwich with bread she'd taken from the freezer—the second loaf they were using—and bacon she had fried. The cost of this little retreat was mounting and that was beginning to trouble Zoe, too. At first, the money she'd intended to leave for the supplies they used was cash she had earmarked for that weekend anyway. A few dollars for gas. A few dollars for food. But now she was forced to dip into the money she was saving for Christmas gifts for Daphne.

And, damn it, that caused a lump to form in her throat. She barely had twenty bucks to spend on her baby. The gifts she could afford would have been nothing but tokens and trinkets. But at least Daphne would have presents under the tree. Now that she and Cooper were eating more bacon than she would use in a year, more coffee than she would drink in a month, and more bread than she'd eat in two weeks, she wouldn't even be able to buy those little things.

Angry, hurt, tired of life tossing her to the ground and stomping on her, Zoe felt her chest tighten, but she swallowed hard and forced air into her lungs. She wasn't a person who fell victim to self-pity. She also wasn't a quitter....

Still, she knew she couldn't possibly be on the right track with her life, or everything wouldn't be going miserably wrong. Her parents had left. Her marriage had failed. She was losing her house. Maybe it was time to realize the common denominator in all these problems was *her.*

She turned away from the kitchen sink and glanced at Cooper, who sat on the sofa in front of the TV, eating his bacon sandwich, mindlessly staring at the morning news. He'd had every bit as many problems as she had. His parents had died young. His brothers had kicked him out of their lives. Yet he hadn't merely survived, he was happy.

Why? Because he'd built a life that couldn't hurt him. True, it was somewhat empty of people, but he was fine. She kept trying to build a life that was full of people, and she consistently got hurt.

She dried her hands on a dishtowel, then leaned against the counter. Facing the prospect of a Christmas without gifts, without cards, without calls from family,

Zoe considered that it was time to face reality. Maybe that was why she had been stranded in the woods with Cooper Bryant. Maybe fate wanted her to see that some people were destined to be alone, and he had entered her life to show her how she should be living, and the kinds of decisions she should be making so she would stop getting hurt.

Still braced against the counter, she crossed her arms on her chest. It seemed logical. God knew Cooper was certainly keeping the upper hand with her. She was the one walking on eggshells, while he controlled the TV and basically did what he wanted. Did she need any more proof that his way of doing things was better?

No. She didn't. But before she would give up her long-held dream of having a family, belonging somewhere, being important to someone, she wanted to know if he really was happy. If his life truly worked for him or if he was just a good actor. And the only way to know if he was genuinely happy was to hear his entire story.

And the only way to hear his story was… Well, she knew his price.

So, before she made any deals with him, she wanted to get some idea whether her theory was correct. And she had a good test for that, too. She marched into the great room before she lost her courage and stopped in front of the sofa, where he sat, legs extended.

She kicked his feet. "Don't you ever think of things like maybe I don't have the cash to pay for everything we're using?"

He didn't even glance up from the television. "I wasn't going to let you pay for everything. I can see that Daphne has her own food and you and I aren't exactly eating an equal amount." He picked up the remote and switched channels. "My thirty bucks would have been right beside your twenty on the table with the note."

"This is going to be more than fifty bucks altogether."

"How much do you think, then?"

"Eighty."

"Plus whatever else we use until the snowplow goes through."

She relaxed somewhat. "Yeah."

"Okay, then. You pay $30 and I'll pay $50."

Well, that was it. Test one. She'd confronted him and he'd hardly reacted, just spit logic back at her. He really was calm. He really didn't stress. He clearly didn't obsess. In lots of ways he made her feel just shy of insane. And that was another thing she was tired of. Always feeling she was nuts, crazy, bonkers because she was reaching for something she would never quite catch.

She drew a breath and blew it out slowly. "Okay, you know what? Things have sort of happened in my head over the past day and I've decided I want to know your family story."

Slowly, as if he couldn't believe what he had just heard, he lifted his gaze until he caught hers. His green eyes glittered. "You know my price."

"Yeah, but, you know, I've never been one to pay full price for anything."

He tilted his head in question. "I'm not sure what you intend to negotiate."

"Well, you put your story out as if it's a big deal. And I've discovered I have a few reasons for wanting to know it. Those reasons have nothing to do with you. I'm doing this because I think I could learn some things from you. But the problem is you could be exaggerating."

He laughed. "Not hardly. My story is good."

"Or," she said, talking over him as if he weren't speaking, "your story could be worthless to me."

His eyes narrowed as he studied her. "What do you think you're going to learn? I'm not Gandhi."

"No, but you are calm. You take life as it comes. The only time I've seen you yell was when you had to convince me to find shelter with you. That means you have a sense of decency and responsibility. But the other things that have happened, well, you seemed to take them in stride. Even caring for Daphne."

He shrugged. "Living life any other way than mine makes it too hard."

"My point exactly. So I want to know how you got where you are to see if it makes sense for me to do the same things."

"And once I tell you my story, we go to bed?"

She took a step back. "Well, that takes us to negotiating again. Like I said, your story may not contain the elements I need to help me."

He shook his head. "Sex is a winner-take-all proposition, Zoe. I tell you the story. We make love. Or we make love and I tell you the story. I don't see any other way to do it."

"Strip poker."

As if he couldn't contain it, a laugh burst from Cooper. "Are you kidding me?"

"Nope." She turned her back on him and walked to the poker table. Suddenly, after six years without support or comfort from her parents and an entire year of missing a husband who really hadn't been worth the time or the effort, she felt very, very calm. "Here's the deal. If I win the hand, you tell me a piece of your story. If you win the hand, I take off a piece of clothing. If I'm naked before your whole story is out, we make love and you finish your story."

But when she pivoted to grab the cards from the credenza and found he was right behind her, her calmness vanished. She always reacted when he was near, but having him so close after propositioning him brought home the reality of what she was suggesting and her breath hitched. He was tall, strong and clearly experienced. She'd been attracted to him from the beginning and if her luck didn't hold there was a good possibility she'd be following through on that attraction. Her nerve endings jumped in anticipation.

"And if my story is finished before you're naked?"

"Then you lose," she said, sliding away from him, forcing herself to be confident again. Exceptional card skills gave her the advantage. If his story was an ego-driven piece of drivel that didn't help her to understand life, she wouldn't hesitate to tell him that. But she didn't think it would be. He had a past every bit as demoralizing as hers and she had a feeling his story would illustrate how he'd risen above it. And she needed to hear that.

"That's why you're so confident. You're sure you're going to win."

She grinned, took a seat across the table from where he stood and began to shuffle the cards. "The same cousins who taught me to shoot a gun taught me to play poker."

"And where are these guys? Should I be worried that you'll call them tomorrow morning and they'll ride up on snowmobiles and beat the living tar out of me?"

She laughed. "No. In case you haven't noticed, there's no cell phone service here. So I can't call anybody. Besides, one cousin moved to Washington, D.C."

"Lobbying against gun control, no doubt," Cooper said as he pulled out a chair and sat.

"The other got married. He's busy with his family."

Cooper tilted his head as if something struck him as odd, so Zoe wasn't surprised when he said, "You told me your parents left you. But what about your aunts and uncles?"

"What about them?"

"Didn't they kind of take over for your parents?"

"No."

"No?"

She sighed. "Look, I'm not a talker when I play cards. So if you think you're going to distract me with chitchat, forget it."

"But you expect me to talk."

"*After* you lose a hand and before we start the next hand."

"You're a prickly little thing about poker." He paused, then glanced up at her. "Unless *you* have something to hide."

She sighed again, disgusted that he wouldn't take her at face value. "My aunts and uncles are busy with their own families. After my parents left I tried to integrate, but there wasn't a whole heck of a lot of room. There are four kids in the one family, six in the other. So I remained an outsider. But that wasn't such a bad thing.

Seeing their family interactions, the closeness, gave me the example of what an ideal family is supposed to be." She took a breath. And maybe that was another problem. Maybe she'd modeled her hopes after families that were the exception to the rule, not the rule.

"But I've been miserable trying to make that system work for me. If I hadn't had that dream of creating the picture-perfect family, if I had stayed single, gone to school, or maybe looked for the *right* guy instead of settling for someone who dazzled me, my life would be different now."

"But you wouldn't have Daphne."

She conceded that with a slight smile. "Yeah. You're right. She's the one good thing that came out of that marriage. But otherwise, the marriage was a huge mistake. My whole life since my parents left has been a series of wrong choices. You, on the other hand, might not be Chuckles the Clown, but you're content. Sometimes that's all we can hope for. That's why I want to hear your story."

With that, she began dealing. "Five-card stud. Nothing wild. Since there are only two of us, let's make it a three-card draw."

"All day? Don't I get a chance to call the game?"

"Five-card stud is pure."

"I still want the chance to call my game."

"Fine. You deal next. You call the game."

"Great."

Cooper picked up his cards and had to work to keep his expression blank when he saw he had two aces. Grinning like a fool was not appropriate in poker. Especially not when the prize was such a good one.

He'd never been given such a wonderful opportunity, and already luck was with him. He couldn't help wondering what piece of clothing she would take off first. Her sweater seemed the obvious place to start.

His collar suddenly felt tight and his nerves began to crackle. He couldn't believe Zoe had caved about sleeping with him, but technically she wasn't caving. She didn't know he was a skilled poker player, so she thought she could win. Still, he understood why she was taking this risk. She was a bundle of emotion and unless she got a poker face for life, people would always take advantage of her. Hadn't he quickly honed in on her weakness and kept the upper hand through their entire stay? The woman needed to toughen up. And it would be his pleasure to help her.

"Draw?"

He lifted his gaze from his cards and caught hers with a steely-eyed look designed to confuse her. "Gimme all three."

She dealt his cards and his serious look crumbled when his eyes nearly fell out of their sockets. He got another ace. Somebody up there really, really liked him. If his luck held, this game would be over in about four hands. Sweater, jeans, bra and panties. His stomach clenched. Four hands seemed like an eternity.

"Since we're not betting, show your cards," she said.

Maintaining as solemn an expression as possible, Cooper set down three aces.

He saw her blink then draw a breath, but otherwise remain calm as she said, "Beats my two kings."

Confidence flooded him. This would be like taking candy from a baby, and he would use her poor choice of poker when he explained his life. He never took a bet he didn't know with absolutely certainty he could win. She'd underestimated him, or overestimated herself. In challenging him to cards, she'd set herself up to lose.

"And I think you owe me a sweater."

"Not yet, cowboy. The first hand gets a sock."

He gaped at her. "Socks? Three aces gets me your socks?"

"I said *sock*."

His eyes widened even further and his mouth fell open. "One damned sock?"

"Well, it seems to me that you probably have a really long story. No sense rushing things."

He studied her for a second, giving her points for keeping control. He hadn't thought she had that in her, but since she'd thrown him into the role of her teacher, he couldn't just let her walk all over him.

"Okay. Fine. If you're insecure about your poker skills, we'll play your way."

"We'll play my way because it's my game. I'm not insecure," she said and proved it by beating him the next hand.

She rested her elbow on the table and after a few seconds of studying him said, "I'd like to hear about your parents."

"I had no say in the sock decision. You get no say in what I tell you. And what I consider to be equal to a sock is this—I have two brothers."

"I already knew that."

"I'd already seen your right foot."

She sighed. "Give me the cards."

She beat him again and this time he told her about

the family construction company. When he beat her, she gave him her second sock. Her ankle bracelet came after her third loss.

"What? Are you going to give me polish chips off your toenails if you lose again?"

She only harrumphed, but she didn't lose again. He did. She was craftier than he gave her credit for, and he worried that the little girl who'd come to him for help dealing with life was about to outwit him. Concluding he was somehow missing an important element about this game, something obvious she was doing to best him, he nonetheless told her that Ty had been old enough to become fifteen-year-old Seth's guardian when their parents were killed.

At the next loss, he admitted that Ty had put him through college.

At the next, he regaled her with a story of how Seth had been a hot commodity with the ladies.

She laughed. "So your younger brother is a sex symbol?"

"We all had our moments with the ladies."

He saw her swallow and was gratified that—at least—she wasn't totally unaffected by him. But none of that would matter if he didn't figure out how she was winning.

She beat him again the next hand and Cooper's head was spinning. Just as she'd said, five-card stud was pure, especially when there was no betting involved so neither one could bluff. Unless she was pulling cards from the bottom of the deck, out-and-out cheating, she had the best luck he'd ever seen.

"I want to know about your moments with the ladies."

"I think my moments with the ladies are irrelevant."

She caught his gaze. "Tell me anyway."

He sighed. "Okay, you won the hand and I'm out of stupid, equal-to-socks things to tell you anyway, so I'm going to give you the equivalent of my shirt."

Her eyes brightened and she leaned across the table eagerly. Cooper's chest tightened. She was so darned beautiful that he knew her ex had to be a total dimwit to leave her. And so darned fresh-faced and enthusiastic, he began to wonder if sleeping with her would be as easy and uncomplicated as he kept all his other liaisons. He hadn't wanted to get to know her. She'd slipped past his defenses. He hadn't wanted to talk to her, yet he was now halfway through his entire life story. He *had* wanted to sleep with her. She was gambling him out of it.

Still he'd promised her something good, so he said, "I once dated the same woman for five years."

Her eyes widened in disbelief. "Are you kidding?"

"Nope. Not kidding." But he was feeling odd. This part of his life story did not paint him in a good light. "Same woman. We weren't in love. Not the passionate, icky, sticky kind that you feel when you're eighteen."

She nodded.

"But…well, I think you need to win another hand to hear the rest."

She groaned. "That's not a shirt's worth!"

"Okay, consider it my wristwatch." He handed the cards to her. "Deal."

Clearly frustrated, she dealt the cards. Cooper didn't think he had a very good hand, but much to his surprise he had better cards than she did.

She passed her wristwatch across the table.

"Very funny."

"Give me something substantial in your next loss and I promise you will get something substantial in mine."

Her statement brought him back to the fact that all he had to do was get her naked and this stupid game would end. He either had to beat her more often, or he had to step up his story so she'd be compelled to remove her more important garments.

He was almost gratified to lose since that gave him the opportunity to tell her something good—and something good should net him, at the very least, her sweater the next time she lost.

"Okay," he said, working to word his next revelation in such a way that it would have value. "My girlfriend called it quits because she told me I'm not very thoughtful. But I think of myself first because that's how I stay on top of things. I might lose a woman here or there, but I don't make any major life mistakes."

Zoe studied him. "Let me get this straight. Your girlfriend put up with you for five years, suddenly called you inconsiderate and left?"

"I'd missed a lot of birthdays. She'd given me a lot of second chances."

"Wow. It sounds like it crushed you."

He shrugged and picked up the cards. "Zoe, that's the whole point. I never let myself invest so much that I get hurt. Life taught me that lesson right off the bat. I lost my parents. I fought almost constantly with my brothers until they asked me to get the hell out of their lives. Losing my parents hurt because I loved them. Losing my brothers hurt because I had trusted them. And they didn't trust me. In fact, they distrusted me so much it was easier for them to lose me than put up with me."

With that Zoe fell silent. And Cooper was damned glad because the god-awful odd feeling was back in the pit of his stomach. He'd never suspected his sparse love life was entwined with losing his family and, frankly, he could have gone the rest of his days without knowing.

Without saying a word, he dealt, looked at his cards, tossed two, and motioned to her to tell him how many she wanted.

"All three."

He dealt her three cards, then gave himself two. Two kings to go with his three sevens. If this wasn't perfect timing, he didn't know what was. Now that the real truth about his life was out, he was determined to start winning so they could move on. To the bedroom.

"Only the strong survive," he said, then caught her gaze and flipped over his hand, revealing his full house. "I intend to survive and I want your sweater."

She turned over her hand. Four nines.

He stared at her. "How the hell do you do that?"

"Once I warm up, I'm lucky at cards." She shrugged. "Lucky at cards. Unlucky at love."

Though he had been gathering the deck, what she said stopped him, and he suddenly knew why she wanted to hear about his life. "You don't want my story. You want to know how to live like me."

"I believe I told you that."

"No, you made it sound as if you wanted my life philosophy but you don't want the generic facts. You want to know my decisions. You want to *copy* my life."

She said nothing, only looked across the table at him.

"Zoe, I'm on the road, have no kids, and have a partner who can back me up…. You *can't* make the decisions I've made."

"Are you saying a girl can't live like that? Because if you are, you should know that I beat my male cousins at cards. I was also a better marksman. And I got better scores on the SATs."

But she hadn't gone to college, likely because her parents deserted her. He and Zoe were comparing apples to oranges. Sure, they had similar pasts in that they had both lost their parents and neither one of them had fit into the life that was left after their parents were gone. But the real reason he lived his life the way he did wasn't a decision—it was an admission that he was untrustworthy. She was about the most trustworthy person he had ever met. There was no reason for her to live like he did. If she copied his life, she would essentially go from being good and reliable to being a relationship schlep like him. He felt like a heel for giving her the idea.

"What do you do for a living?"

She shook her head. "Nice try. But you lost the hand. So you're the one who's supposed to be talking."

He drew a frustrated breath. She had a baby. She needed to be soft and sweet and honorable. This was all wrong. Even having an afternoon fling with her suddenly seemed horribly, horribly wrong.

He swore he heard his hormones groan, but he knew it was true and he knew he had to stop this right now. "My fight with my brothers began over a woman."

One of her eyebrows rose. "Really?"

"My brother Ty, the oldest, was engaged. His fiancée

ran around on him all the time, but I didn't tell him until she hit on me."

"Holy cow!" Her eyes widened in disbelief and Cooper realized he had a quick way to end this game, the conversation, even their bet.

"You want to hear about some more cows? My brother had already taken the family business much further than my parents ever dreamed. Anita was a gold digger. Ty had money and she wanted it."

Her eyes widened to the size of saucers. "Your family had money?"

"Ty made Bryant Construction into Bryant Development. He's probably worth a billion dollars right now."

"You left *billions of dollars?*"

"No, when I left we were only millionaires."

"You're a millionaire?"

He shook his head. "No. I washed my hands of it."

"Are you insane?" She rose from the poker table with her eyes flashing fire. "Every month I wonder whether or not I'm going to have enough money to pay my utilities. This fall, I got a notice from the county that my parents haven't been paying the taxes on my house. I'm going to lose it soon because after so many years of unpaid taxes the county can sell a piece of real estate right out from under anybody living there."

"Money isn't everything."

His quiet statement seemed to bring her back to earth and she shook her head and sat again. He had expected her to storm out of the room. Instead she grabbed the cards. The game was still on.

Anger ripped through Cooper. Under normal circumstances hearing that someone was about to lose her house would have made him think the involved person was a nitwit who couldn't keep up with life. But having felt the sting of betrayal after reading the letter from his brothers' attorney, he knew that sometimes some people really were innocent victims.

This woman was about as innocent as they came and he would *not* be the one to ruin her.

"Why don't *you* pay the taxes?"

Calm again, she shuffled the cards. "I didn't realize they were going unpaid. I was eighteen when my parents left. Which means six years have gone by. When I got the notice that the taxes were so far behind, I called my dad, and found out he had paid for a few years but he'd felt it was my mother's responsibility to pay for a few years."

"And your mother?"

"My mother was busy. She couldn't believe I had called her. She said that since she didn't live in the house, she had no reason to be responsible for the taxes and hung up the phone."

"Oh."

"Don't," she said, holding up her hand to stop the flow of sympathy he could feel ebbing from himself and which she undoubtedly could feel as well. "After I got off the phone, I realized she was right. I'm twenty-four years old. I shouldn't be calling my mommy to bail me out. Since I'm the one living at the house those taxes are my responsibility."

She drew a quick breath. "Unfortunately, with the penalties and interest that have accrued, I owe so much I can't even get a loan for the amount. But even if I could, I couldn't afford the loan payments. I'm a clerk at a grocery store. The only thing that has made it possible for me to live on my own and support a child is that I have a house and haven't had to pay rent." She paused and sighed. "But we're talking about me again."

"And I told you something equal to your win." Not sure what else to do, Cooper ran his hand along the back of his neck. "If you want more info you need to beat me again."

She dealt. He lost. He was beginning to believe she really was cursed to being lucky at cards, unlucky at love.

"Frankly, Zoe, I'm out of things to tell you."

She looked him in the eye. "Tell me how to do it. Tell me how to stay sane, how to get the attitude that I should only look out for myself, how to resist the temptation to try one more time to get somebody to love me."

He couldn't handle the sadness in her pretty blue eyes, so he focused on the other point of her question. "Is that how you see me? As somebody who only looks out for himself?"

"Isn't that how you see yourself?"

Yes and no. He looked out for himself because he was strong, able, independent. Somebody avoiding pain. Not somebody intent on hurting people. Not somebody who was selfish. She saw him as selfish.

He cleared his throat. "No. That's not how I see myself. And you win. My story is over and you're fully clothed. You don't have to go to bed with me."

Chapter Seven

Cooper couldn't sleep that night. He tried to tell himself that the difference between being inconsiderate and selfish was small and he had accepted himself as inconsiderate, which made him an idiot to care about being called selfish. But it didn't work.

There *wasn't* a small difference between inconsiderate and selfish. There was a pool. A swimming pool. An *Olympic* swimming pool. Inconsiderate people didn't see things, didn't think things through. Selfish people were *deliberately* self-centered. They saw others' needs and ignored them.

Pacing, Cooper tried to remember when he'd seen one of Bonnie's needs and ignored it, but he couldn't recall a time because there wasn't a time. He simply, honest-to-God had never seen what she needed.

He didn't believe that made him a bad person. He thought being inconsiderate made him unfit for relationships. And he accepted that. Hell, he had recognized that as part of the deal back when Seth had kicked him out of the house. He was who he was. Since he couldn't change, he chose to keep his distance from people who couldn't tolerate him as he was.

Except Zoe didn't think that he was inconsiderate. She thought he was selfish.

He fell to the bed and groaned. Damn it! Why did he care?

Because she was a smart woman. She'd seen so much of life he could tell she was a good judge of character. She wasn't just a pretty girl or a sexy woman. She had a real heart. And if she thought being selfish kept him sane and she decided to imitate him, she would lose that heart.

But, he *wasn't* selfish. He was thick, obtuse...or overworked. Burdened with his own problems.

He combed his fingers through his hair. Actually, that *was* the gist of it. When he was with Ty and Seth, his burden had been to do his share of work needed to make Bryant Development great. Ty was a genius planner. Seth was a networker. Cooper was the guy who got things done. While his brothers made deals, Cooper oversaw the resultant projects. Yes, he was tough. But being the voice of the company at the job sites was not an easy task. He took it seriously. It was a responsibility...a burden of sorts. It had hurt that his brothers hadn't seen his value, had only seen him as trouble.

Then after Seth had asked him to leave, his burden had become starting over from scratch and making something of himself. Alone. No money. No contacts. No help. And he'd done that. Until they'd bought his mortgage.

Now his burden had become trying to hold on to the ranch—and not for himself, for his partner. If he failed to get the mortgage money to his brothers' lawyer on time, his partner, Dave, would lose the money he'd invested, too.

There was no way Cooper would let that happen. So, Zoe Montgomery was wrong. He wasn't selfish.

He was who he was.

But if he didn't somehow make her understand the difference between being burdened and being selfish, she was going to imitate all the wrong things and it would be his fault.

That was the part of the situation that made him the most angry. He stayed out of other people's lives not merely because he was inconsiderate, but also because he always screwed things up when he got involved. Now, he would have to fix the impression he'd unwittingly given Zoe.

The only way he could do that would be to talk to her again and if he talked to her again, there was a possibility he'd make a bigger mess of things. Worse, there was also the possibility that he'd like her even more than he already did. He'd fought it and fought it and fought it, but the woman was just plain nice and funny and pretty. But he was trouble. The absolute last thing she needed in her life was a man like him.

The next morning, Zoe awakened feeling miserable. Now that Cooper Bryant had gotten to know her, even he didn't want to sleep with her. Could a woman get any lower? Sure, he'd tried to pretend he'd lost the bet, but it was abundantly clear to Zoe that he hadn't so much *lost the bet* as he'd *lost interest.* He'd heard her story and metaphorically run for his life.

She slipped out of bed, changed Daphne, then took her to the kitchen for some cereal and a bottle. She made a pot of coffee and toast but Cooper still didn't come downstairs. With a sigh, Zoe put Daphne on the blanket on the floor in the center of the great room, turned on the TV and sunk on to the sofa.

After an hour, Daphne played herself out and fell asleep on the comforter, but there was still no sound from Cooper. Zoe turned and peered up the stairs. She suspected Cooper was avoiding contact with her, but it seemed odd he hadn't come down for coffee. She walked to the French doors to stare outside and suddenly realized that the second storm had stopped. It was even somewhat sunny.

A horrible thought paralyzed her. The snowplow could have come through the night before. If it had, Cooper could have gone.

And why wouldn't he? The details of her life had made him uncomfortable. So uncomfortable, he couldn't even bring himself to sleep with her. If he'd heard the snowplow in the middle of the night he could have taken advantage of the opportunity to skip out.

Something inside Zoe snapped. After four days of being stuck together, he hadn't even had the decency to say goodbye. Was anybody ever going to stick with her to the end of anything?

Wanting to confirm her worst fear so she could get really angry and stop being such a schmuck about people, Zoe bounded up the steps. When she reached the top, she turned into the bedroom she knew Cooper was using and stopped dead in her tracks.

He wasn't gone. He was still asleep.

She took another step into the room. Seeing him tucked under the covers sent a shaft of pure, unadulterated relief through her, but it also confused her. Not once during their stay had he slept in. More than that, even if the snowplow hadn't gone through last night, both she and Cooper expected it to come by today sometime. He should be up and packing, or, at the very least, pacing, dying to leave.

She walked to the bed and peered down at his face. Oh, Lord! His cheeks were red. His brow was dewy with fever-induced sweat. She and her daughter had both exposed him to their virus. She squeezed her eyes shut in misery. She shouldn't be surprised he had caught it, too. But that didn't stop the guilt that spiraled through her. She had been nothing but trouble to this man.

She shook his shoulder. "Cooper?"

He mumbled.

"Cooper, I want you to get up and come downstairs so you can sleep in the bedroom with the bathroom."

He mumbled again.

"That's the spirit," she said, knowing his mumble didn't necessarily mean he was alert, but at least he was awake. She gingerly began to lift the blanket so he could climb out of bed. "Come on. I'll help you walk."

"I'm fine." He took the cover from her hand and put it back where it had been. "I know I have what you and Daphne had. I also know it's smarter to be in the bedroom with the bathroom. But I'm…well, naked under these covers."

She stepped back.

He sort of laughed. "I'm harmless, but I still have my pride. Leave. I'll be down."

Zoe did as he said. Telling herself not to dwell on the fact that she had nearly seen him naked, she ran to the bedroom she was using and quickly gathered Daphne's things. By the time she was done, Cooper was at the bottom of the steps. Though he had put on jeans and a T-shirt, he was also wrapped in the blanket from his bed.

"Just go ahead in and go back to sleep. Daphne and I will be as quiet as we can."

"Great," he rasped, then stumbled into the room.

He closed the door behind him, and Zoe breathed a sigh of relief. But when three hours passed without hearing a sound from him, she decided to make sure he was okay. She sneaked into the room and placed her hand on his forehead. It was hot, but he was sleeping soundly and there wasn't anything she could do for him, so she left.

In the great room she paced, watched TV, then paced some more before she fed Daphne lunch and played with her. When Daphne fell asleep in her drawer, Zoe sneaked into the bedroom again to look in on Cooper. Though he slept soundly and there was no reason to stay in the room, Zoe stood by his bed, mesmerized.

His face was still shiny with fever, and his dark hair was disheveled from a restless sleep, but he was still the most handsome man Zoe had ever seen. She had nearly fainted when he'd kissed her. And, yeah, he was grumpy and self-centred, but he had a kind heart. Whether it was smart or not she liked him.

She took a quick breath. She liked him a lot. That was why she had been so troubled when she'd thought he had left without saying goodbye. Though he tried to pretend he was *The Grinch Who Stole Christmas,* deep down inside he was a good guy. In his story of his life, she had seen a man who had faced adversity and won. She had seen a man who still respected the very brothers who didn't want him around. She had seen a man who was genuine and honest. Even the way he'd stopped the poker game the day before proved he had integrity. Unfortunately, it also quite clearly said he didn't feel about her what she was realizing she felt about him.

Confused by how she could be letting herself fall for another man whose feelings didn't match hers, she sat on the edge of the bed. When her weight shifted the mattress, he opened his eyes and she smiled. "You're up."

"If you want to call it that."

Trying not to succumb to guilt over being the one who had given him the virus, she laid her hand across his forehead. "You feel a little hotter than I remember being."

"I'm fine."

"I'm sure you are, but it still worries me."

He laughed.

"You think it's funny that I worry?" she asked, knowing darned well he thought her a sap and knowing as well as he did that she was going to have to change.

"No, I do not think it's funny that you worry. I was just trying to recall," he said, his voice slow and tired, "the last person who worried about me." He took a breath. "This is the other side of that life of mine that you're trying to learn to copy. This is the empty side." He caught her hand and his weary eyes held hers. "This is what you don't want, Zoe. It's okay for me to be alone. I know how to nurse myself through illnesses that come along. I can entertain myself on lonely nights. I don't need a breakfast companion. But I don't think it would be okay for you."

She looked down at his hand holding hers. Strong callused fingers gripped hers firmly, as if he wanted to be certain she paid attention. But there was also comfort in the gesture, and a strange notion occurred to her. She'd thought he'd stopped the poker game because he was no longer interested in sleeping with her, but what if the conversation had caused him to see enough about her that he was beginning to like her the same way she liked him? He'd appeared angry, but what if that was because he'd recognized he was starting to care about her and he didn't want to?

She stared at their joined hands. Now that he had her attention, he could let her hand go, yet he didn't. It seemed odd that he would allow himself such a quiet gesture of affection, but she realized he might be too sick to fight his feelings. Maybe too sick to understand that something so sweet and simple as holding her hand meant a hundred times more to her than his wonderful, deep kiss had.

"And another thing," he said quietly, then swallowed as if the slight conversation was exhausting him. "Don't get all invested in the idea that you need to be selfish. That's just going to ruin your life."

Her eyes filled with tears. He *did* care. He cared enough to fight his own need to sleep to prevent her from making a mistake. However, she wasn't kidding herself. Cooper was also a loner and loners didn't hang around to help sort through problems. He might like her enough to clear up a misinterpretation, but he wasn't the kind of guy who would work with her to fix what she had done wrong.

All the same, she'd reached her limit. Living her life longing for something she was never going to get was killing her. At the very least, it was killing her spirit.

"I've got to do something, Cooper," she said, staring at their entwined fingers, wishing he were different, wishing he would stay, yet knowing if he were anybody but the stubborn, quiet, determined guy she was coming to know she wouldn't feel the same about him. She liked that he stood his ground, knew his mind, only went after what he wanted. Even though that also meant he stayed away from her.

"I'm sort of breaking. You know how everybody has that point where they can't keep up what they're doing anymore because it's hurting more than helping? That's where I am."

"You've got to find a way to keep going."

She shook her head. "I'm out of ways."

He took a breath and closed his eyes. "When I feel better, we'll brainstorm."

She smiled. "Right."

"I mean it."

His reply came out so slow and sluggish, Zoe knew it would only be a matter of seconds before he drifted off to sleep again. But he still had hold of her hand.

The pool of tears in her eyes expanded to overflowing. Whether he knew it or not, Cooper Bryant had real feelings for her. And she, well, she was falling in love with him.

"Why don't you stay in my life and help me figure out what I'm supposed to be doing?" she asked, half hoping he had fallen asleep because she suspected she already knew the answer. He might have feelings for her, but he didn't want them. He liked his life free of responsibilities. Women in general were a responsibility for men. But a woman with a baby and a past was a burden.

"I'm not the best person to help you figure out anything." He drew a tired breath. "Besides, I don't have time."

"Have you ever tried making time?"

"Did I neglect to tell you about Bonnie?"

Zoe laughed. The fact that he compared her to an old girlfriend, not his brothers, not his partner, not a friend, was very telling and it gave her the courage to be honest. "Things between us would be different. I would be smart enough to know to give you space. I would know how to live with you, Cooper. I wouldn't get in your way."

When he didn't reply, Zoe couldn't tell if he didn't argue because he'd fallen asleep, or if he was actually considering what she had said.

In case he was thinking about it, she pushed on. "You know...we have a built-in opportunity to see if we could have something because the sheriff is selling my parents' house." A new idea came to her and she blurted it out before she could stop herself. "I could move to Texas with you and stay with you until I got on my feet."

But even as she said the words, Zoe knew she wouldn't be staying with him until she got on her feet. She was already halfway in love with him. She would be totally in love with him after a few weeks of living with him. And she knew she'd spend those weeks desperately trying to make him love her.

Unfortunately, she also knew he'd be in his home territory and he could slide back into his routine and easily ignore her. Worse, he could end up wondering what the hell had possessed him to let her move to Texas with him. Assuming he even let her go with him at all.

Her suggestion of moving to Texas with him would only work if she could get him to realize right now, while they were still stuck in Pennsylvania together, that he wanted more from her than something casual.

Recognizing he was asleep by his deep breathing, Zoe rose from the bed. But when she reached the door she stopped. She felt better.

A lot better.

Almost as if she had hope in her life again.

In the great room, she peered into the drawer to make sure Daphne was still napping, then she sat on the sofa and analyzed what had happened in that bedroom. She couldn't feel hope about her feelings for Cooper. He'd probably fallen asleep before she'd made her suggestion about Texas, but if he hadn't, he had ignored it. When he was well again, he could yell at her for even asking. So she knew her unexpected infusion of well-being had not come from him.

She thought about everything they had said in those few minutes of conversation. When that reaped no results, she focused only on what *she* had said and she suddenly realized that buried in their discussion was her admission that the county sheriff would be selling her house.

She gasped softly. Whether she'd intended it or not, in that short discussion, she had let her house go.

She leaned back on the couch and closed her eyes. The truth was the house might come with free rent, but it was an albatross. It cost too much to heat. The roof needed to be patched. The faucets leaked. The furnace was on its last leg. Maybe that was why it didn't hurt to let it go.

Even if Cooper Bryant didn't want her, she was going to be okay. She and Daphne wouldn't end up on the street. They'd end up in an apartment, probably shared with someone she'd find through a newspaper ad. And her new roommate could be good company. Who knew? She might end up with a best friend…or someone who could become as close as a sister.

That thought intensified the hope she felt. But she heard a sound from the bedroom and spun to face the closed door.

The idea of a sisterlike roommate did give her some sense of a happy future, but she'd much, much rather move to Texas. Still, she couldn't be the one to bring it up again. She'd given Cooper plenty of hints that she would be willing to start something with him. But more than that, she couldn't say or do anything that would cause him to put up those walls again. She had maybe one more day before Cooper would leave and she wasn't going to ruin the chance that he might see the obvious for himself.

Cooper awakened at around four o'clock in the morning. Realizing his virus had run its course, he pushed himself out of bed. Though there was a bit of residual stiffness, he no longer felt he could throw up. He no longer felt weak. All of this was very good news.

He pulled on the jeans and T-shirt he had dropped at the side of the bed, then went in search of his boots. He found them, shoved his feet inside, grabbed his jacket and left the house. From the porch he looked out at the moonlight glistening off the packed snow. The air was crisp and clean. The world was a silent winter wonderland, and he let himself absorb the peace before he jogged down the steps and headed for the driveway.

The other good news of the morning was that in spite of his fever-induced delirium, he remembered talking with Zoe about selfishness. He didn't recall exactly what he had said, but he knew he had made his point that selfishness wasn't the way to go. Even though she'd argued a bit about needing to change something in her life, Cooper had no doubt she wouldn't take the selfish route because she was a smart woman. She would be okay. And that meant he had to leave before he did any more damage to her fine, upstanding set of morals.

With the moon lighting his way, Cooper walked out to the road. When he saw it hadn't yet been plowed, he sighed. But he also understood that the state had been busy clearing the main arteries. He was sure this road would fall into the department of transportation's radar some time within the next twenty-four hours and he and Zoe could go their separate ways.

All he had to do was behave himself for about sixteen more hours and he wouldn't have to worry that he'd ruined a perfectly sweet woman.

He trudged back to the cabin and glanced at his wristwatch. It was nearly five o'clock and he knew that Daphne usually woke before six o'clock, so after stripping off his denim jacket, he went into the kitchen and put on a pot of coffee. He watched it brew, then drank a cup, letting the minutes tick away until five-thirty, when he began frying bacon.

Around ten till six, the sounds of Daphne's whimpers and wake-up cries drifted down the steps. At five till six, Zoe padded into the kitchen with Daphne.

"Good morning."

This was where he hit the dilemma. If he wasn't at least polite, Zoe would go back to believing the selfishness theory he had hoped he had wiped clean yesterday. But if he was too nice, she would get all the wrong ideas…. He stopped his thoughts. It might be true that Zoe was coming to like him as much as he feared he liked her, but once they left this house it wouldn't matter if Zoe thought she was head over heels in love with him. They would never see each other again. It was better to err on the side of caution.

He smiled. "Good morning."

"I see you're feeling better."

"A hundred percent better. But you probably know exactly how I feel since you had the same thing."

She smiled. "Yeah."

"Listen, why don't you let me feed Daphne while you go shower? I know what it's like to be her keeper for twenty-four straight hours, so I know you could use a break."

She licked her lips. "Really?"

"Sure." He'd expected a more joyful reaction, not something so analytical, and he concluded he must not have gotten his point across the day before. Knowing he couldn't let her leave this house with the wrong idea, he decided he had more explaining to do. "I remember talking yesterday about selfishness—"

Her eyes widened. "You remember our conversation from yesterday?"

"Yes, and I want to make sure you got my message. I don't want you thinking that by becoming selfish you can make your life better. You can't."

She frowned, then slowly asked, "That's all you remember?"

"Yeah," he said, but he searched her eyes. He experienced the usual slam in the gut that he always got when he looked into their blue depths, but this time he saw something that made him realize their conversation had gone a lot further. And whatever they'd discussed, it was important.

"What else did I say?"

Taking a step back, she licked her lips. "Nothing," she said, but a current of electricity passed between them. More than attraction, it hinted that they'd come to an understanding…or something.

His eyes narrowed. "What else did *you* say?"

She drew a breath.

"Zoe?"

She sighed. "It's not important. Really."

He studied her for a second, feeling a strength of connection to her that had no basis. Finally, he said, "I think it is. I think I must have given you another wrong impression about me and I'd like the chance to fix it."

She sighed again. "All right. What if I tell you this? You didn't give me any wrong impressions."

"I think I did. It isn't just your behavior. I *feel* something—"

"Damn it!" she said, interrupting him. "You just aren't going to let this go, are you?"

"No."

"All right, then, here's the deal. We had a really nice

conversation because you were too sick to argue. You even held my hand. So I got brave enough to ask if I could come live with you when the sheriff sells my house."

He frowned as the words began to sink in. Now that she mentioned it, he remembered holding her hand and how right it had felt. He remembered drifting off to sleep picturing her in the house on his ranch. Picturing her with the horses. Picturing her in his bed.

A shaft of white-hot desire shot through him, but he ignored it in favor of getting to the truth. "You asked to live with me…." He closed his eyes and realized what had happened. He'd been too weak to fight his feelings, and she'd seen them.

Unwilling to let her hope for another thing she couldn't have, he shook his head. "Zoe, do not even go there."

Her chin lifted. "Why not? It's my life and—"

"That's exactly the point. This is your life and you're not the kind of girl to live with someone!"

"How do you know that when I don't even know that for sure?"

"*I know,*" he said, getting angry now. She might not have been a virgin when he met her, but Zoe Montgomery was pure. Not the vague kind of pure people associate with sexuality, but pure about life. She wanted life's best. In less than a week, he'd corrupted her.

He headed for the door. "I'm going outside to see if the snowplow came through." He knew it hadn't but she didn't know he knew. "When I get back there'll be no more talk of living together! You're too good for that, Zoe," he said, slamming the door behind him.

Chapter Eight

Midmorning another snowstorm hit. For two solid hours Zoe held Daphne on her lap and stared out the window. She reminded herself that even though Cooper Bryant didn't want her, she could get a roommate. She also told herself that once she got rid of her albatross house, she could get loans and grants and go to school, and eventually land a job that paid well. Things were not *that* bleak. So what if Cooper Bryant didn't want her to live with him? She hardly knew the man.

Daphne made a whimpering sound. As if by rote, Zoe rose from her seat, warmed a bottle, fed her baby and laid her in the baby drawer in the bedroom. Because the sides of the drawer were high enough, she could let Daphne sleep in it without worry that she'd get out, and she acknowledged to herself that Cooper was quite inventive when he wanted to be.

She stopped her thoughts and squeezed her eyes shut.

She had to quit thinking about him and giving him credit that he didn't deserve. Yes, he had found somewhere for Daphne to sleep, but he'd done that for his own sanity. Everything he did, he did for himself. He was not nice. He was not thoughtful. If he came up with creative solutions they were to save himself work or ease his conscience. He was *not* the kind of man she wanted to fall in love with, and if it killed her, she was getting over her feelings for him.

Daphne fell asleep. Zoe left the bedroom and walked to the window again. Staring at the big fat flakes as they fell was similar to watching a train wreck. She didn't want to stay another day with Cooper. Yet, for some reason or another, fate had chosen to torture her.

Finally, she decided to indulge herself in her only real activity. Showering. She forced herself away from the window and her gaze collided with Cooper, who lay on the sofa engrossed in an old movie.

She would tell him she was about to take a shower, but she knew he didn't give a damn. He didn't give a damn about anything. That was why he wasn't upset and stressing over the new storm as she was. That was why he could contentedly watch a movie. He didn't invest any emotion in anything—especially not her. No. Not just her. People in general. He didn't expect anything or give too much, and she needed to start doing that, too.

She left the great room, made a quick check on napping Daphne and headed for the shower. She was sure the dull ache in her chest would go away eventually. But for now it wasn't budging.

She sluggishly showered, then stepped out and unenthusiastically toweled her hair until it was dry enough that she could put on her day-old sweater. She shimmied into her already worn jeans and ran a finger full of toothpaste over her teeth, then ambled into the bedroom again.

Unfortunately, when she glanced into the baby drawer, Daphne was nowhere around and all the self-pity in which Zoe had indulged vanished with the violent pump of her heart. Her baby was gone!

She looked around the bedroom, including under the bed, in case Daphne had crawled out of the drawer and had gotten herself stuck there, but she didn't find her little girl. Panicked now, she scrambled out into the hall between the kitchen and great room. Immediately, she saw Daphne's baby seat on the kitchen table, happy baby inside.

"What is she doing out here?"

Cooper shrugged. "I promised to take her this morning, but I went outside. So when I heard her cry, I got her."

Zoe noticed that his answer was simple, to the point, and that he was gathering cans from the cupboard as if he were about to make something for lunch.

She walked to the table. "Come on, Daph—"

Cooper half turned from the counter. "Leave her. We're fine."

Righteous indignation rose up in her. She was *not* accepting any more of his charity. And if he didn't really care about her as a person, then anything he did for her was charity. Or a way to make it palatable to have her around, and Zoe didn't like that, either.

"I don't need your charity."

He shook his head with disgust. "I'm not giving you charity."

"Okay," she said, as pride and anger straightened her spine, "then what would you call it?"

"How about charity for Daphne. She doesn't need a grouchy mother."

Zoe took a sharp breath. He could call her a prude. He could call her stupid. He could call her insane for all she cared. But he could not call her a bad mother. And he knew that. He knew her vulnerable spot and he'd hit it.

Cooper cursed softly. "Sorry. That came out wrong."

Zoe didn't believe it had. Thinking back to everything they'd been through in the past few days, she realized part of the reason Cooper was so good at taking care of himself was that he took things at face value. He didn't read anything into any situation. He dealt only with facts, logic and reason. And the "fact" was he hadn't called her a bad mother. She'd read that into his comment. He'd said she was grouchy. And she *was* grouchy. She couldn't take offense at the truth.

An unexpected sense of calm enveloped her. Using logic and reason really seemed to work.

She took a step back from the table. "Don't worry about it. I *am* grouchy and feeling sorry for myself and all kinds of other stupid things. So maybe I do need a few minutes alone. Though I'm not sure what it'll accomplish." She combed her fingers through her hair. "I wish I had a book…or more space to pace in. I wish I could stop the world long enough to clear up a few of my problems." She smiled uneasily. "But I can't. So maybe a few minutes alone will make me feel better."

"Why don't you put your coat on and go for a walk?"

She laughed and shook her head. Texas boy. Thought it would be fun to walk in the snow. She showed him her tennis shoes. "If I walk in two feet of snow in these, I'll ruin them."

He shrugged. "Sit on the porch. Some days when I feel the weight of my problems, I sit on my porch and look out at how big the world is and realize I'm sort of small and in the grand scheme of things my problems are small and I feel better."

She nodded. Having already made a fool of herself in front of this man, she decided not to argue with his advice or mention that his sentiment was awfully poetic for a man who was so pragmatic. Instead, she walked into her bedroom and put on her insubstantial red leather jacket. Knowing that wouldn't be enough to fend off the cold, she took a blanket from her bed, walked through the hall and front door and sat on the top step of the porch.

And for some reason or another, maybe it was because she was alone in a pristine world, or maybe because she felt as insignificant as Cooper had suggested she would, she suddenly found herself smack-dab up against the truth of why she was so upset. She didn't care about her house. She didn't care about money. She didn't even care about apartments or going to college. She was lonely and tired of being alone. And she thought somebody like Cooper Bryant, who had been deserted by his family and more or less shoved aside by life, would understand that and see her as the answer to his loneliness, too. But he didn't.

Cooper looked out the window and seeing Zoe cry made his chest hurt so much he almost couldn't breathe.

Daphne wailed.

He turned toward the kitchen where he'd left the

baby in her travel seat and saw Zoe's energetic daughter slapping her chubby hands against her sausage-like thighs. He pulled her from her seat and instead of grabbing his nose, pulling his hair, or twisting his lips, Daphne cuddled into his neck.

He squeezed his eyes shut. It almost seemed that if one of these two Montgomery girls didn't get to him, the other did. Daphne was sweet and fun. Zoe was sexy and determined. And life was simply kicking the heck out of them. First, Daphne's dad had left. Now, Zoe's parents had let the taxes go unpaid on the only break life had given her.

Daphne snuggled against his shoulder and he sighed heavily. There was no way in hell he was letting his two girls suffer. He couldn't change Zoe's life. He couldn't change that her parents had left her or that her ex-husband was an idiot. Yet he wanted to do something. He *had* to do something! He couldn't let life beat her down anymore. He and Zoe might have both lost their parents at eighteen, but he hadn't been left alone. Ty had made sure he had gone to college. Then, even after he left his brothers, fate had been kind to him in finding him a partner. No one had ever done anything for Zoe.

So he had to. But what? Cuddling Daphne as he paced, Cooper racked his brain and suddenly the answer came to him. So simple. So clear. He could pay the taxes on her house. Actually, if he gave her the certified check he'd had prepared to pay off his brothers, he wouldn't be merely paying the taxes on her house. He would essentially be handing her four years of college tuition and support for those years so she could go from poverty to a normal life.

It meant facing his brothers.

No, it meant facing his brothers as a failure. No check. No explanation. Just the simple admission that he couldn't pay the mortgage, so they could foreclose. Seeing him humbled was what they wanted. They didn't want his ranch. His brother had more money and material objects than they knew what to do with. But that was good because that meant he could take care of his partner.

His brothers' lawyer's letter had said that if he couldn't pay the mortgage balance before December 24, he had to tell Ty face-to-face. If he were the only one losing the ranch, he would have ignored that provision, but because he had a partner who stood to lose everything he'd invested, Cooper intended to accommodate it. He would go and see his brother Ty, all right. But it wouldn't be to grovel as he expected was Ty's intent in that provision. No, he would demand a check for the equity he and his partner had earned on the ranch, so Dave wouldn't lose his investment.

Then, Cooper would continue driving truck and saving, and in a few years he would have another down payment for another ranch.

So he could give Zoe his check. Not because he was a saint. And not because he wasn't selfish. But because for him, starting over wasn't all that hard. He'd played this out once. He knew what to do. Zoe, on the other hand, was trapped and he simply could not stand by and do nothing.

But now that he'd gotten her back up, there was a good possibility she would refuse his "charity" and he had to figure out a way to get her to accept the money. Today's snowfall had granted him the grace of one more day before he and Zoe would be heading home. But it was only one day, so he had to do something quickly. Something he knew she couldn't resist. Unfortunately, the only thing she couldn't resist was him.

He didn't want to give her the wrong idea, but this time tomorrow she'd be in her house on the other side of this godforsaken mountain and he'd be on his way to Texas. Short of seducing her, he had to do whatever it took to get her to accept the check.

When Zoe entered the front foyer, her tears were dry. She blamed her red nose on the cold and happily took Daphne from Cooper's arms, swearing that the hour and a half outside was exactly what she needed.

He sighed with relief. "Great. I fed Daphne a bottle. Why don't you put her down for her nap, catch a nap yourself, and maybe fix yourself up a bit?"

She gave him a confused look.

"I made a special stew for supper and I just thought it would be nice…." He kicked the toe of his boot along the linoleum. "Ah, damn it, Zoe. Look, this storm isn't like the last one. It's passing through. The roads will be cleared late tonight or early tomorrow. We're going to be leaving and there are some things we need to discuss." He paused and caught her gaze. "I think I've figured out a way to solve your problems."

"You have?"

He shrugged. "Yeah, but I don't want to talk about it right now. We both said things we didn't mean this morning and it made me think about you and your life and I have a proposition for you. So you go take a nap and fix yourself up and I'll check on the road conditions and finish dinner. Then while we're eating I can make my proposal."

She drew a long breath. "Let's just talk about it now."

He put his arm around her shoulder and guided her to her bedroom. "No. Daphne needs a nap and I want to check on the road conditions to be sure the road crews really will get to us tonight or tomorrow. And I don't want to rush this. I want it to be special."

He walked away. Zoe stood frozen for a few seconds, then spun to watch his retreating back.

Special?

And hadn't he used the word proposal?

Yes, but he'd also used the word proposition. It was totally out of the realm of possibility that he would ask her to marry him. But it wasn't so far-fetched to consider that maybe he wasn't going to leave her…. Maybe he'd decided to let her come to Texas with him!

Zoe had never felt her spirits lift so fast. One second her heart was in the black pit of despair, the next it was on the highest mountain singing for joy. From their argument that morning she knew he wouldn't want her to "live with him" in the conventional sense, but because of that argument she also knew he thought of her as someone special. He liked her. And if she went to Texas with him it would only be a matter of time before he loved her.

She put Daphne down for her afternoon nap and then slipped up the steps in search of an attic. Cooper was in freshly laundered clothes. She'd worn the same two sweaters and pants for days. True, she had laundered them, but she was tired of them. She wanted to wear something pretty. And her only shot at something pretty would be finding some discards in the attic that she could somehow mix and match to make herself look and feel beautiful.

But the attic was filled with old hunting jackets, vests and smelly boots. She almost believed she was going to have to be Scarlett O'Hara and make a ball gown out of drapes, when at the back of the attic she saw a trunk. Everything inside looked to be from the forties, and, sadly, everything exceptionally pretty or dressy enough to be worthy of a special dinner was also made from wool. Because everything in the trunk smelled funny, anything she wanted to wear would have to be washed, and that counted out all the wool clothes.

Then suddenly she saw a simple, sleeveless white cotton dress sprinkled with purple violets. It was sweet and feminine and could be laundered. She grabbed it and ran down the steps to the basement where she tossed the garment into the washer. She waited until the cycle was finished, then brought the dress upstairs. But rather than dry it in the great room, where Cooper could see it, she hung it on a hanger from the curtain rod in her bedroom, right above the furnace vent. Within two hours it was dry. Then she showered, put on makeup and slid into the dress.

When she walked out of her bedroom, all the lights had been dimmed and the television had been tuned to an all-music channel. Soft rock glided through the air. Daphne happily played in the dresser drawer in the center of the great room floor.

At the kitchen table, Cooper glanced up from cutting a chicken and said, "Oh. Well…" He paused as his eyes took a slow inventory. Then he swallowed. "Don't you look nice."

She smiled. "Thanks."

Fighting a serious case of butterflies, she walked into the kitchen. Because she didn't have shoes that complemented the dress, she wasn't wearing any. Barefoot and in the airy sleeveless dress, she probably looked like a woman about to go on a picnic with her lover, rather than a woman stranded in a cabin in the middle of a cluster of snowstorms.

She saw Cooper swallow again. "You *really* look nice."

And Cooper felt *really* funny. If he still had a stomach it had fallen to the floor. He couldn't stop staring at her, but when he noticed it was beginning to make her uncomfortable he reminded himself that he had to get her in an amiable enough mood to take his check.

The gentleman he usually kept buried rose up in him and pulled out her chair.

She smiled. "Thanks."

Zoe made dinner very easy. She kept her voice low, her comments quiet and Cooper relaxed, knowing softspoken, quiet Zoe could be persuaded to accept the money. She wasn't the arguer or the spitfire. She was the woman with common sense. The check was as good as in her bank account.

But as quickly as he realized that, sadness enveloped him. He might succeed in putting the money in her hands, but he also knew they weren't going to see each other again. He longed for a kiss. One more kiss. A kiss to remember…

He glanced at her, thinking how pretty she looked,

how innocent, and reality intruded. Their attraction was much too potent to risk another kiss.

Still, he wanted something special to make this a night they could both remember. A slow romantic tune floated from the television and, inspired, Cooper rose. "Would you like to dance?"

She smiled shyly and agreed and Cooper's heart did a somersault. He couldn't believe everything was going so smoothly. He'd thought for sure she would immediately demand to know his proposition. Instead, she seemed to want to make this night as memorable as he did.

As he pulled her into his arms and began to glide around the floor, he realized again how well they fit together. The warmth of her pressed against him felt so wonderful, so natural, he couldn't help admitting that though they might not be perfect partners, they did have "something." He had no idea what it was, but there was clearly a connection between them. Swaying in rhythm with the soft music, they both knew it. And she probably wanted a kiss as much as he did.

Unable to resist, he lowered his head and kissed her. As always, the world spun. But this time it didn't tilt off its axis. This time he understood the sexual attraction had been seasoned with genuine affection and he enjoyed it because it was the last kiss he would get from her, or give her. This was the end for them. Except he had to give her his check.

Compelled by the truth of that, he pulled away. There would never be a more perfect moment. He slid his hands from her waist so he could clasp her fingers and said, "Zoe, I know we haven't known each other very long, but we'd be foolish if we didn't acknowledge that in these past few days we've become very close."

She nodded.

"We've shared a lot of things about our lives that I'm guessing we've never shared with anyone else."

"Yes."

He drew a quiet breath. "So, I want you to have my check."

She blinked. "Your check?"

"Yes." He pulled the folded white envelope out of his back pocket. "This is the certified check I had written to pay off my brothers. It's more than enough to pay the taxes on your house and probably put you through all four years of college. I want you to have it."

She searched his face. "This is what you wanted to talk about tonight?"

"Yes." He opened her hand and placed the envelope in her palm.

She looked at it, then caught his gaze, tears shimmering on her eyelashes. "This is really it? All of it? Everything you wanted to tell me?"

Panic gripped him. He expected her to be overcome with joy or to get angry. He didn't know how to deal with questions or confusion. "Yes."

Holding his gaze, she asked, "So, what was the kiss all about?"

He cleared his throat. "Zoe, you're kind of an irresistible force and we're friends…."

"So, that kiss meant we're friends?"

He studied her for a few seconds, then said, "We're more than friends. And you know that. I wouldn't be giving you my life savings if we weren't."

"But we have no future together."

"We've been through this. I can't commit. If you knew me better—"

"We know each other well enough for you to give me every cent of money you have, but you think we don't know each other?"

He shook his head in disbelief. "You expect to be bosom buddies after six days?"

"No, I expected you to like me enough to want me to go with you."

His eyes widened. "Come with me?"

"Yes. To Texas. I'm losing my house, remember?"

"That's why I'm giving you the check."

"I don't want your check! I want you to love me!"

"*Love you?* In six days?"

"You're giving me every cent of money you have after only knowing me a few days. To me it makes as much sense to think we could fall in love, as it does to give each other our bank accounts."

"You need this money more than I do. I can start over, but you…"

Eyes flashing fire, she said, "I what?"

"You have a baby."

Cooper watched Zoe force herself to be calm. "I know we haven't spent a lot of time together, but you should have known better than this." She stuffed the check into his shirt pocket. "I told you. I don't want your charity."

With that she walked out of the room, and Cooper stood flabbergasted. She'd missed the significance of what he had done. He hadn't merely given her every cent he had. He was willing to give up years of his life for her. But she didn't want what he was offering.

She wanted him to love her. *Love* her. Even if he were the kind of guy to fall head over heels, he wouldn't do it in six days.

This really was the end.

Chapter Nine

The mood in the house the next morning was black. Cooper didn't know whether to be astounded that Zoe could possibly think he could love her in a matter of days, or angry that she'd thrown his generosity back in his face.

When she came into the kitchen and silently gathered Daphne's assorted bottles and half-eaten jars of baby food, her beautiful yellow hair cascading around her, his mind nearly took off in a direction that he knew it wasn't wise to go, so he focused on his anger. She needed that money. Hell, *he* needed that money. But he was giving it to her because her need was greater. That money was her jump start to life.

But she didn't want it because she'd fallen into some starry-eyed vat of stupidity and thought he should love her. Yes, she was beautiful. Yes, he'd love to make love to her. And, yes, under different circumstances—for instance if they lived anywhere near each other—they might be friends. For him, even admitting he wanted to be friends was a stretch. But they didn't live close enough that there was a hope in hell they could maintain a friendship. What would they do? Talk on the phone? Yeah, like he'd spend hours chatting!

But she didn't even want to be friends. She wanted to be lovers. In a real relationship. And she thought they were already on that road. Because the thing left unspoken the night before was that she loved him...or thought she did.

Which astounded him. Even if he did believe in love, even if he believed somebody could love him, there was absolutely no way in hell he would accept that somebody could fall in love with *anybody* in less than a week. Period. So she didn't love him and he sure as hell didn't love her.

She left the room as silently as she had entered and Cooper wilted. He didn't love her. But he did care about her. He cared about Daphne. And he knew enough about life to realize that Zoe had been given a raw deal. He also knew enough about life to suspect that he'd been thrown in her path at the very time that he had a cashier's check because his money was actually supposed to be *her* money. And he knew enough about life to realize that things didn't happen by accident. He'd met her, come to care about her, so he could give her the leg up she needed because he'd already proven that when the chips were down, he could always find a way to save himself.

He frowned. Did that mean he thought she *couldn't* find a way? Was that why she was so angry?

He almost slapped his forehead at his stupidity. He most certainly did not think she couldn't find her own way. He believed she was smart and capable but over-burdened. He believed that his money would give her the chance to get the education that would allow her to live the way she was supposed to live. He also believed that if she were by herself, with no baby, no day care, no formula, diapers, or wipes to buy, she would kick life's butt.

But the circumstances were that she had a baby and unusual expenses and she needed a break.

Still, if she assumed he'd offered his herd money because he thought she *couldn't* save herself…well, then he supposed he understood why she was upset. Which simply meant he had to explain that she had taken his offer the wrong way. And once he explained she would see he didn't think her stupid or lazy or incompetent, simply overburdened, she would take his money.

Relief overwhelmed him and he walked into the bedroom where she was stuffing Daphne into her snowsuit.

"Can I talk to you?"

"I think we said everything that needed to be said last night."

"Now, see, there's where you're wrong. Because out there in that kitchen, after only a few seconds of real thought, I realized why you're mad at me. And if we had talked a few minutes longer last night, all this," he said, waving his hands around her room to indicate her quick packing and silent departure, "would be unnecessary."

She turned from the bed, holding grinning Daphne, and pushed past him to the door. "I have to get home."

"And I have to get on the road, too," he agreed, following her. "But this is an easy thing to settle. I figured out that you're mad at me because you think I'm giving you my mortgage money because I think you can't make it on your own. But the truth is," he continued, speaking quickly because she was rapidly striding to the door, "I don't think you're incapable. I think you're overburdened. I think life dealt you a bad hand, and even with your poker skills, it's killing you."

She put Daphne in her baby carrier and set it on the floor in the hall, then turned and ran into Cooper.

She sighed. "Move. I need to get the diaper bag."

"Why don't you let me get the diaper bag?"

"Because I can handle everything myself!"

Her words hit him like a slap across the face, making him see he was right on the money with his assumption that he'd insulted her, so he pushed on. "Yes. You *can* handle everything yourself. That's my point."

She shifted and walked past him to the bedroom. He scrambled after her.

"I'm not giving you my money because I don't think you can handle things. I'm giving you the money because I know you can. With this money you will get a degree—you will have money for both tuition and day care and living expenses for the years it will take. Then you will get a job and become self-sufficient. To me you are a good investment."

"I'm an investment?"

From the tone of her voice, he couldn't tell if she thought that a good or bad thing so he went with the truth. "Yes."

Her eyes narrowed. "So, you want the money back eventually?"

"No! It's not a loan."

"Right, because if it was a loan you would have to give me your address so I could make payments and you don't want me to have your address."

She was right. He didn't like people knowing where he was. He didn't like being accountable or depended upon. He just wanted to give her the damned money.

"Why is it so hard for you to believe that somebody wants to *give* you something?"

"Because no one's ever given me anything! There are always strings attached. There's always a catch."

"This money comes with no catch."

"Except that it gets me out of your hair. This way you leave me without regret. You won't love me. You say you can't, but I say you *won't*. So you give me your money, take the burden of sacrifice on yourself, don't have to worry about me, don't have to think about me…except maybe to have a warm feeling in your heart to know you gave me everything you had." She paused. Her gaze caught his. "But you're not giving me everything you have. I want *you*. You want to take the easy way out. Buy me off. Ease your conscience." She drew a quick breath. "Well, I won't let you. I want you to think about me. I want you to remember me. I want you to know that without you I'm alone and struggling."

The thought of her being alone, broke, hungry, cold, nearly did him in. Until he realized that was exactly what she wanted. She wanted him to feel he somehow was to blame for that. Just as Seth blamed him for the Bryant brothers not getting along. Just like Bonnie blamed him for their relationship fizzling. He cursed. "Take the money."

She grabbed the diaper bag and hoisted it to her shoulder. "No. If you really believe I'm strong, you know I don't need it."

She stormed to the front hall where Daphne sat trying to shove her entire fist into her mouth. Zoe grabbed the carrier handle, adjusted the diaper bag onto her back and headed for the door. But the weight of the diaper bag shifted and she nearly fell.

Cooper sighed. "Let me carry the diaper bag."

With her back to him, she tilted her head back and drew a deep breath. He knew she was debating. He knew she hated to look weak. Because she wasn't weak. But she needed help. He suddenly felt her pain, her burden. How would it feel to be a strong, self-sufficient person, who suddenly needed help? He couldn't imagine it because he'd never needed help. Life had always given him the resources to save himself.

He slowly walked to the door and eased the diaper bag from her shoulders. "No strings attached," he said quietly and opened the door, motioning with his hand for her to go out.

She nodded. He pulled the door closed behind them and followed her, watching her walk, back straight, head held high, to the driveway. His heart constricted. She was so proud. He could feel her pain. He knew she would never let him talk her into taking his money. But now that he was holding her diaper bag, he didn't have to talk her into taking it. He could simply give it to her.

He stopped walking. "Hey, Zoe. I just realized there's no point in me walking this twice. I'm going to run inside and get my duffel and backpack. You keep walking. I'll catch up."

She nodded. He breathed a sigh of relief and ran back to the house. He grabbed his duffel and backpack, which were in the great room where he'd stored them while he'd gone out and shoveled around his truck and her car to assure they weren't plowed in. He unzipped the backpack, pulled out the check and stuffed it into Daphne's diaper bag. Zoe would find it when she dumped the bag to do the laundry.

She'd probably curse him.

She'd probably almost tear up the check at least three times over the course of a long week that she'd spend looking at it.

But he would bet every cent of money in this check that ultimately she'd cash it…because betting every cent of the money was exactly what he was doing. It was a certified check. If she didn't cash it, the money was lost to both of them.

Zoe trudged up the mountain to her car. She remembered making the suggestion to Cooper the day they were stranded that they walk downhill rather than uphill looking for a cabin. At the time, she'd been so engrossed in his thunderstruck reaction to her touching him that she hadn't thought about how walking down to find shelter meant they would have to walk uphill to return to their vehicles.

She took a quick breath. "We're fine, Daphne," she told the baby girl who seemed happy to finally be outside in the fresh air, even if that air was only about thirty degrees. "We survived when your dad left. We'll survive now."

Daphne cooed and Zoe lifted the carrier high enough that she could nuzzle Daphne's face and grin at her daughter. But she knew her smile didn't reach her eyes. She had survived without Brad because Brad was a loser. He was a narcissistic boy. And every time Zoe missed him, if only his companionship, she reminded herself that there was somebody better out there. But she couldn't do that with Cooper because he was her some-body better. Even the way he'd tried to give her his check proved he was unselfish. Kind. Caring. But he didn't see it. Nope, unlike Brad, who only saw his good and never even considered he might do things wrong, Cooper only saw his faults. His mistakes. And he couldn't believe he would ever do anything right, good or kind.

He thought she was the one life had overburdened, but Cooper was the one who would always be trapped. He would always be alone because the person he refused to trust was himself. That knowledge hurt her worse than realizing she might always be alone because she didn't believe anybody would ever compare to him.

She heard the crunch of snow behind her and realized Cooper was catching up to her. So she put on a brave face. She didn't want his memories to be of her angry with him. After all, he might have decided to live without her, but she most certainly intended to haunt his dreams.

He skidded to a stop beside her. "See, I told you I could catch up."

She smiled. "Yeah. I figured you would."

He adjusted her diaper bag and his backpack on his shoulder and started walking again.

"I don't want us to end on a sour note," she said quietly, hesitantly, because she wasn't sure how this comment would be greeted. But they were only about ten feet from her car. Ten feet of time left together. Ten feet to tell him the things she wanted to say. So it had to come out right.

"I didn't like us leaving mad, either."

She took a quick breath, then smiled at him. "Good, because I never got a chance to say what I wanted to say last night." She took another breath. "I think you're a very, very good person."

He looked away. "Yeah, well, you've got some stars in your eyes."

"And you're too hard on yourself."

Surprisingly, he laughed. "You aren't going to give this up, are you?"

She shook her head. "I have about five more seconds," she said, stopping by her car. She opened the door and slid Daphne's carrier to the driver's seat. Because Cooper had let her car run while he'd shoveled, the inside was warm. She lifted Daphne from the seat and buckled her into her car seat. She gurgled happily.

"Daphne's glad to be going," Cooper said, nodding inside the car.

"Want to say goodbye?"

He swallowed and looked away again and Zoe's heart broke. He didn't even see that it was more painful for him to avoid love than it was to risk loving.

"Go ahead," she urged, nudging him toward the open door of her car. "Just poke your head in and say goodbye."

He nodded and bent inside her car. "Hey, kid. You be good."

She screeched and slapped his nose with her rattle.

Zoe winced, but he laughed as he pulled out of her car. "She still loves me."

His words shot an arrow in Zoe's heart. She knew he didn't mean them literally, only as an expression, so she smiled and said, "A slap with the rattle is her highest praise."

He nodded, stepped back. "So…you take care of yourself, okay?"

She nodded, and glanced to the right as misery tumbled through her. Damn it. She couldn't believe he could let it end like this. Especially since she couldn't! Before he knew what she intended to do, she took a step forward, grabbed the lapels of his jacket and pulled him to her. Standing on her tiptoes, she kissed him. At first he didn't respond, and then as if he couldn't help himself, he wrapped his arms around her, jerked her closer and deepened the kiss.

But he quickly pulled away and they stared into each other's eyes.

Please, she thought. *Please don't let me go. If nothing else, ask for my address, my phone number…anything!*

But Cooper stepped back. "Be careful going down the hill."

"I'm going up, remember?" she whispered. "I live on the other side of this mountain," she hinted, giving him the chance to say, "Yeah, where on the other side of the mountain?"

But he said nothing. Walking backward, he held her gaze for a few seconds.

Inspiration struck Zoe. "I could give you a ride up the hill to your truck—"

He shook his head. "No. I'm okay. I've been cooped up for so long the walk will feel good."

She nodded.

"Get into the car, Zoe."

Her chest tightened.

He turned away.

Zoe slid onto the driver's seat. The car spun a little as she edged out onto the road, but eventually the wheels caught and she was on her way. Up the hill. Home.

She passed Cooper. He didn't look at her. Didn't wave. Eyes straight head, he continued up the hill. All by himself. Because that's the way he liked it.

A few times she let her gaze stray to the rearview mirror. She memorized his long stride, the straightness of his spine, the sheer determination in his posture and carriage.

She was never going to get over him.

Chapter Ten

Cooper was surprised by the address Bryant Development's attorney had given him for Ty's home. He had expected his successful older brother to have purchased an ostentatious mansion to showcase his wealth and good fortune. Instead, Ty apparently still lived in the old family home where he and his brothers had started their lives.

Familiar with the streets of Porter, which he noted hadn't changed much in eight years, Cooper easily found the house and pulled into the driveway. Overwhelmed with memories, he sat in his four-wheel-drive truck, staring at the front porch, remembering other Christmas Eves.

He could hear his parents' laughter. Remember the gleam in their eyes because there were always Christmas secrets and surprises. Sadness enveloped him. Their parents would be so disappointed in the angry way he and his brothers had parted. They would be even more upset that Cooper, Ty and Seth didn't speak. If it weren't for the mortgage, Cooper wouldn't even be here right now. If it weren't for Zoe, he most certainly wouldn't be civil. But Zoe had changed him. If nothing else, he had to acknowledge that.

He walked up the sidewalk and, rather than take the turn that would lead him to the front porch, out of habit, he ended up at the kitchen door.

A gorgeous redhead answered his knock. "Merry Christmas!" she said.

Cooper cleared his throat. "Merry Christmas," he parroted, if only out of politeness. He felt like an idiot for having waited until he was down to the wire on the deadline, but really hadn't had much choice because of being stranded. His brothers would simply have to accept that explanation, and, if not, Cooper wasn't sure it mattered anyway. They had his mortgage, which meant they had his ranch. There wasn't too much more that could be said about that. "I'm sorry. I think I came at a bad time. Explain to my brothers that I'll come back to talk about the mortgage the day after tomorrow—"

The redhead's mouth fell open. She gasped, "Explain to your *brothers?* Are you Cooper?"

He shuffled his feet. "Yeah. But this looks like a really bad time so I—"

She grabbed his forearm and hauled him into the house. "Oh, no you don't!" She quickly closed the door behind him. "Ty!"

Embarrassed to the tips of his boot toes, Cooper glanced around. The kitchen was much cleaner than he remembered, but otherwise little else had changed. It was as if Ty had decided to preserve the hub of the house exactly as it was.

"I'm Madelyn, Ty's fiancée." She smiled. "I don't know what the holdup with Ty is, but I do know he wants to see you."

Cooper smiled wryly. "Right."

Madelyn put her hand on his forearm again. "No. Really."

Another minute ticked off the clock and Cooper glanced at the door.

"He probably didn't hear me," Madelyn said. "Keep an eye on Sabrina, will you?" she said, pointing at a little girl sitting in a high chair who looked about a year old. "I'll go check things out."

Two weeks ago, that request would have filled him with fear. No, two weeks ago the request that he stay with a baby would have sent him running. Today, after having spent almost a week with Daphne, he said, "No problem."

When Madelyn was gone, the little girl screeched at him, banging her hand on her high chair tray.

Cooper approached the high chair. "What's the matter, kid? Haven't they fed you?"

She bellowed, revealing two bottom teeth and one top.

Cooper laughed. "Damn, you're a cutie—"

"She's Scotty's daughter. Scotty and his wife, Misty, were killed this summer in a boating accident. I got custody."

Cooper spun away from the table to see his brother Ty. Dressed in a forest-green sweater, with the collar of a white shirt exposed, and wearing black trousers,

Cooper's dark-haired, dark-eyed brother looked the picture of wealth and sophistication.

Wishing with all his heart that he hadn't come, but knowing he had to stay to get Dave's equity, Cooper quietly said, "Hello, Ty."

"Cooper," Ty said, inclining his head. "Seth's on the way over. I called him when I saw you get out of your truck."

Cooper raised his eyebrows.

"I heard it pull in. Nothing gets by me anymore."

Point for Ty. Apparently his cheating fiancée, Anita, had taught him a lesson or two.

"Let's go back to the den," Ty said as Madelyn entered the kitchen. "Miss Maddy, would you mind making coffee?" He paused and faced Cooper. "Unless you'd like something else."

"Since I'll be driving back to Texas tonight, coffee would be best."

Cooper watched Ty and Madelyn exchange a look. Ty appeared lost. Madelyn's expression egged him on. *Go,* her eyes seemed to say. *Go.*

They arrived in the den. Ty directed Cooper to sit on the brown leather sofa. He took a seat on the wing chair, but the doorbell rang and he rose again. "That will be Seth."

Cooper said nothing. Ty left the room and within seconds, he was back, Seth on his heels. Dressed very similarly to Ty in trousers and a cable-knit sweater, Cooper's pale-haired, green-eyed brother Seth also looked like a man with money. Cooper glanced down at his worn jeans, his battered boots. He hadn't deliberately dressed to celebrate his poverty. He hadn't dressed to make his brothers see the differences in his status. Boots and jeans were who he was now. Ty and Seth might be sweater guys, but Cooper was a boots guy. He raised cattle. He rode fence. He mucked stalls. Luckily, he didn't do any of those in these boots.

And also, luckily, he remembered some of the things Zoe had told him. That deep down inside he was good. Which meant he didn't have to apologize to anyone for who he was.

He rose from the sofa and extended his hand to Seth. To hell with it. If they wanted his ranch, they could have it. But he wasn't begging for Dave's money. He would demand it. He would go down with his dignity.

"Hello, Seth," he said, as Seth took his hand.

"Cooper."

"Let's sit," Ty said, his natural leading abilities taking over. Cooper prepared himself for an argument, but no matter what his brothers decided, he would be as Zoe saw him. He would be strong. He would keep his dignity. His pride.

"Cooper, we're sorry it took the drastic measure of buying your mortgage to get you here."

"Actually," Seth cut in, "it wasn't even our idea. My father-in-law thought of it. He's…well, he's more accustomed to persuading people to do his bidding and he knows a few more tricks than we do."

Cooper looked at his younger brother. "What are you talking about?"

Ty laughed. "Cooper, your idiot brother married a princess. His father-in-law is the king of a small country called Xavier Island. It's off the coast of Spain."

Cooper couldn't help it. He laughed. "Are you kidding?" He glanced from Seth to Ty. "You are kidding, right? This is an icebreaker?"

Seth shook his head. "No. It isn't an icebreaker. I married Lucy knowing she was a princess, but I hadn't thought it was a big deal...until I saw her in action, doing her 'royal duties.'"

"Now, he has to attend royal ceremonies...ride in a carriage..." Ty chuckled, "wave at his subjects."

Seth growled. "Shut up, Ty. I've been to Xavier three times and never once have I waved from a carriage."

"But it's in the cards," Ty said, laughing again.

Cooper glanced from one to the other and suddenly felt eighteen again. The need to tease welled up in his chest so strong and so fierce he couldn't resist it. "Are they going to make him wear purple tights?"

Ty howled with mirth. Seth scowled. "No one wears purple tights. You guys are remembering something from one of mom's old storybooks."

"Right," Ty said.

Cooper grinned. "Right."

Ty took a quick breath. "Okay. We can tease Seth anytime. We need to get down to business."

Cooper's chest tightened. *Dignity,* he reminded himself.

Ty reached behind him to retrieve a manila envelope and handed it to Cooper. "Here's your mortgage. Burn it. Frame it. Shred it. We don't care. It's yours. I'm not a hundred percent sure what happened that caused us to break apart, but I want us back together again."

"And I also want to say I'm sorry," Seth said, jumping in as if worried that he would lose courage. "I was a kid. I shouldn't have said the things I said, and I knew I was wrong two hours after I said them, but by then you were gone."

Cooper stared at the envelope in his hands.

"You also own one third of our company," Ty said. "Seth and I both take salaries for the work we do, but we keep that separate from actual ownership and profit sharing at the end of our fiscal year.

"Profits aren't always high," Ty continued, "because we pour a lot of money back into the company. We've expanded several times so your company shares are worth more than the profits, but you've gotten anywhere from a few hundred thousand dollars to close to a million every year."

Cooper felt his eyes widen. "Close to a *million?*"

"You're rich," Seth said simply. "You shouldn't have a mortgage. When King Alfredo was investigating me he discovered you, and your mortgage. He forgot about it until he found out from Lucy that we wanted to talk to you. Then, he bought the mortgage and gave it to me as a wedding present, suggesting we use it to lure you here so we could tell you about the money you have so you can fix up that ranch of yours."

"Unless you want to move back and work with us," Ty quickly interjected.

Stunned, Cooper looked at him. "Work with you?"

Seth raised his hands. "If you don't want to, that's fine, too."

"But you have a degree in business," Ty reminded him. "And you would fit in perfectly." He paused. "And this company is your heritage as much as it is ours."

"This is it?" Cooper asked, waving his mortgage and

looking from brother to brother. "This is why you brought me home?"

Ty and Seth exchanged a glance. "Yes."

"You're not kicking me off my ranch?"

Seth laughed. "No. My God, if King Alfredo dies, Lucy and I are literally responsible for a country until our son Owen is old enough to take over. We don't want any more land, thank you very much!"

"And I have my hands full. So full," Ty said, "that I could use some help."

Cooper stared at him. "Just like that?"

"Just like what?" Ty asked.

"You would take me into your company, give me an upper echelon job, without even knowing me."

"We know you," Ty said. "You're one of us. You're family. We all had things to work out, but that's over now. From today we accept each other as we are and work as a team."

And that was that. Ty told Cooper he had as long as he wanted to make up his mind about working for Bryant Development. A job would always await him. But if he wanted to join the company sooner that would be great since Ty wanted to take an extended honeymoon with Madelyn the following summer. Seth said his wife and his son had come with him when he'd driven over, and they were in the kitchen waiting to meet Cooper. And Ty said that Cooper really hadn't been properly introduced to Madelyn.

The next thing Cooper knew he was in the kitchen. Madelyn's parents had arrived with a baked ham and plates filled with Christmas cookies. He met Prince Owen, Seth's baby son and future king of Xavier Island,

and stunning Princess Lucy, and understood why Seth had married her before he'd really thought about the whole purple tights issue. He met Madelyn's two brothers and sister, and so many neighbors arrived that the kitchen rapidly filled with people and the party spilled over into the family room.

For the first time in eight years Cooper was in a house with a Christmas tree. A ham. Cookies. Eggnog. For the first time in eight years he heard carols sung, by family, simply for the joy of it, and he leaned against the doorframe between the family room and kitchen, taking it all in.

He now had everything Zoe wanted.

Chapter Eleven

Cooper stood on the porch of Zoe's small house, not quite sure what he was doing in freezing cold Pennsylvania again. He knocked on the door then blew on his hands before he stuffed them into his pockets.

Zoe opened the door, holding Daphne, who was dressed in red reindeer pajamas. Zoe's glorious blond hair was rumpled. Her jeans were threadbare. Her sweatshirt appeared to have seen more washings than all of Cooper's clothes put together.

She looked wonderful.

"I hope you've come for your check, because I didn't cash it."

"Actually, I didn't." He paused and glanced at the toe of his boot. He knew he was using her and he knew that wasn't right, but he had nowhere else to go. No one else to turn to. "Zoe, I need somebody to talk to."

He raised his head and caught her gaze in time to see her eyes soften with compassion. "What happened?"

"My brothers put a provision in their letter that if I couldn't pay off my mortgage I had to meet face-to-face with them. I thought it was a good idea since I intended to get my partner's equity, but—"

Zoe grabbed his arm and yanked him inside. "Don't stand there on the porch freezing, Arkansas boy. Come in."

He grinned. "I thought you'd never ask."

"Don't mind the mess," she said, kicking Christmas wrapping paper out of the way and Cooper suddenly realized he'd interrupted their celebration.

"I'm sorry," he said, backing away. "I should have thought a little bit about what day it is."

She batted her hand in dismissal. "My celebration is over. My mother called. My dad and his new wife sent a plant." She shook her head. "I didn't even know he was getting married. Hell, I didn't even know he was dating someone. Anyway, Daphne has opened her gifts. For me Christmas is over."

Cooper's heart squeezed with pain. The night before he'd been welcomed with open arms into his family. He'd had an elaborate dinner. He'd eaten homemade cookies, met relatives, been invited to parties. A private plane had brought him to Pennsylvania. "I met a prince."

She turned and smiled. "What?"

"A prince. My younger brother is married to a princess."

Zoe's face lit with happy confusion. "A princess?"

"Her father is the king of an island country."

"Wow!"

"Zoe, that's only the tip of the iceberg. Little Owen may someday be a king, but Ty's already the head of an empire. When I left, the development company was booming but my two brothers have turned it into something that I never envisioned."

"Well, you knew they were rich to be able to buy your mortgage."

"Actually, the king bought that for Seth as a wedding gift."

Zoe grinned, sliding Daphne into a high chair. "What a hoot."

Cooper shook his head. "Ty is marrying a woman who is the public relations director for his company. Her parents and half the neighbors are fixtures in my brother's home."

Zoe sat at the table. She braced her elbows on the place mat in front of her and her chin on her fists and smiled at him. Nobody had ever looked so good to her, or so sad. He had absolutely no idea of what he wanted out of life, because he'd never been allowed to keep anything. His parents had been killed. His brothers had more or less kicked him out of their lives.

"Lots of family."

He nodded. "Lots of family."

"Does that scare you?"

He shrugged. "I was treated as if I had never gone away."

"As if it never happened?"

"No," Cooper quickly said. "Ty and Seth both apologized." He smiled ruefully. "Then they handed me my mortgage, told me to burn it if I want." He shook his head. "I was the one who made the trouble and they apologized to me."

"And…"

"And I wanted to tell them I was at fault, too, but I couldn't. I didn't get time. Before I knew it, we left the den and they introduced me to the rest of the family and suddenly I had a beer in my hand and people were opening gifts and shoving cookies at me." He paused, swallowed. "I never realized how lonely I was."

"Ah."

"Or how empty my life was."

"You filled your time with work. Running a ranch and driving truck." She smiled. "Two jobs. Not much free time."

He shook his head. "No."

"Cooper, you just need a few months to adjust."

He looked at her hopefully. "Really? You think that's it?"

Unfortunately, she did. She had wanted to believe in her heart of hearts that Cooper was here because he finally realized he had fallen in love with her the way she had with him, but there were so many other things going on in his life that she knew he hadn't. When they'd met he was preoccupied with the fear that if he didn't get his money to Arkansas he would lose the one thing he had worked his whole life for: his ranch. Instead his brothers had handed him his mortgage. Welcomed him with open arms. Given him a family.

Now, he really had no reason to want her in his life. She was as good as out. Her throat tightened from wanting to cry, but she wouldn't. She refused.

"And they offered me a job."

"Really?"

"I think I could do anything I want at Bryant Development since I own one-third of the company. They've been putting away my share of the profits ever since I left."

And he's rich, too. Great. Now he was really out of her league.

"That's wonderful." She paused, then said, "So why are you here?"

"I'm here because I realized last night that I now have everything you wanted."

"And you feel sorry for me?"

"No! Hell no!" The truth was he had no idea what he felt for her. But whatever it was, it had made his chest ache the night before. When he thought of her, he got hot and cold. He hated that she suffered. He believed she belonged on a pedestal. He knew she could fit in with his family. He believed his family should be hers.

He would give her the moon if he could, and though he knew that financially he could buy her just about anything, personally he had nothing to offer.

"I feel like my family should be your family. They are everything you deserve."

"You came here because you want to give me a family?"

"Don't you understand?" Cooper bounced from his chair at the table. "I have nothing to offer you! You need the real thing. You need a man of character and courage who can stand by you. Someone who will love you forever not just 'while he can.'"

Zoe stared at him. "You don't think it took a man of great character to give me his cashier's check?"

"That was only common sense."

"And you don't think it took great courage to go to Arkansas to meet with your brothers—not for yourself, but so you could demand the ranch equity for your partner?"

"I might agree with that, except I had everything about the situation wrong. They didn't want the ranch."

"You didn't know that. You went there with your head held high, ready to argue for your partner, and ready to start over again because you are strong. You are about the strongest man I know, Cooper Bryant. And why you don't see that I will never know."

He knew she believed everything she was telling him. He had even drawn on her belief in him the night before. But today, sitting in her kitchen, reconciled with his brothers, with more options open to him than at any other point in his life, he realized that none of it had any meaning without her. He suddenly saw that the reason he believed his family should be her family wasn't because she needed them but because he needed…no, wanted…just plain *wanted* her with him.

She brightened his day.

She made him see truth.

She believed in him.

She made him laugh.

She made him angry.

She had done what no one had accomplished in eight long years. She made him *feel.* For Cooper, years of emptiness slid away. Years of self-doubt crumbled. Years of needing to prove himself spiraled into nothing.

And he smiled, then he chuckled, then he out-and-out laughed. "Zoe Montgomery, you are the pushiest female on the face of the earth."

"You need to be pushed."

He caught her hand and pulled her out of her chair and into his arms. "Of course I do."

"Occasionally you need someone to tell you what to do."

"Occasionally." He tightened his hold. "But what I just realized I needed more than anything else was for someone to teach me to feel again."

She pulled back and stared at him.

"When my brothers kicked me out, I turned off my emotions. But you, with your strip poker, your virus, your insistence on washing your clothes and your ever present baby…well, you didn't give me two minutes to turn anything off. I couldn't stop my emotions from pouring out and they all did. I felt more with you and for you in those days stranded on the mountain than I had in eight years and if I hadn't met you before I went to see my brothers I would have stonewalled them. I never would have accepted their apologies let alone their generosity. I owe everything I have today to you."

"Well, you were pretty closed off."

"And rude."

She nodded. "And rude."

"And I think that's why I'm here."

"To tell me you're not going to be rude anymore."

He shook his head. "No."

Her eyes narrowed. "Well, it better not be to give me more money because, damn it, I don't want your money!"

"It will look pretty darned foolish for my wife to refuse my money."

She thought about that a second, then her eyes widened. "What are you saying?"

"I'm saying we should get married."

She gaped at him. "Married?"

"And move to Arkansas."

"Arkansas?"

"Where it's warmer."

She stared at him.

"And where you can meet my brothers and Madelyn and Lucy…and Prince Owen and Captain Bunny—"

"Captain Bunny?"

"Ty's future mother-in-law. It's a long story."

"You and your brother call his future mother-in-law Captain Bunny?"

"Because he's part of her family and her family has become my family." He stopped and his heart swelled. He had something to give Zoe beyond money, beyond even his love. "Say yes and you instantly have a family."

She took a breath. "I want a family, but I also want to make clear that if I choose to marry you it wouldn't be for a family." She took another breath. "It would be because I love you."

And Cooper suddenly realized what he was doing wrong. Why she wasn't jumping for joy and accepting his proposal.

"I love you, too," he said and allowed himself several seconds simply to soak in the fact that he'd actually said that and meant it.

He now had a family to offer Zoe. More than himself. Two brothers. Two sisters-in-law. Two children. A family. A legacy.

But more than that, he was giving her his love.

"So you'll marry me?"

She leaped into his arms. "Yes!"

Epilogue

The following June, Zoe slowly made her way up the aisle of the small country church, holding her bridesmaid bouquet and smiling at the crowd. She and Cooper had beaten Madelyn and Ty to the altar because neither she nor Cooper had wanted a big wedding. Both had been alone so long they were eager to be together and didn't wish to wait the months it would take to plan an elaborate event. Instead, they'd simply surprised Ty, Madelyn, Lucy and Seth with a trip to Las Vegas where Cooper's family had witnessed the wedding of Cooper and Zoe. Madelyn had put the wedding announcement in the paper while the happy couple had honeymooned.

They'd returned in time for Cooper to handle an unexpected problem with the delivery of some materials to a construction site and Cooper had been working with his brothers as a traffic manager ever since. His partner now ran the ranch, which had a full herd and employed ten hands. Zoe had paid the back taxes on the house, but called her parents and told them it was their responsibility to sell it or rent it, and her parents had agreed to call each other about the matter. She and Cooper had bought a huge home in Porter where Daphne had become good friends with Sabrina and Owen.

Making her way to the altar, Zoe smiled at Cooper, then Seth, then Ty, who waited impatiently for Madelyn. All three men looked wonderful in their black tuxes and to see them no one would ever have guessed that the three brothers had been estranged for eight long years. They were happy.... No, they were tight. Like three men who defied anyone who would try to come between them. Exactly the way Zoe believed brothers should be.

From there she cast a quick glance at Daphne, who was in the arms of Mildred Jenkins, Seth's next-door neighbor. Daphne was happily patting Mildred's face, but Mildred hardly noticed because she was too busy peering over the crowd, hoping for a peek at the bride. In the seat in front of Mildred, King Alfredo appeared oblivious to little Owen's singing, as he, too, craned his neck to see the bride. And in the seat in front of the king, Audrey Olsen, Princess Lucy's best friend, held squirming Sabrina and also angled her head to catch sight of Madelyn.

Zoe had discovered she had access to a nanny brigade, friends of Madelyn's mom who didn't merely babysit, they would also make meals and give lessons on anything from cooking to gardening to baby care…as long as you joined their card club and didn't mind getting your butt whopped in pinochle.

At last, Zoe reached her spot at the altar beside Princess Lucy, who looked regal and stunning in the simple green gown Madelyn had chosen for both her bridesmaids.

In her spot at the altar, Zoe turned. The organist changed tunes, and at the back of the church Madelyn and her dad, a short man with a graying crew cut, stood in the doorway. Though Zoe had seen Madelyn a hundred times that morning, she couldn't stop her eyes from misting. Madelyn was the perfect bride with her red hair pulled into a cluster of curls at the top of her head and a veil that made a tulle backdrop for her bare shoulders and sequined gown. Her full skirt swished as she walked. And her smile could have charmed the angels.

Zoe noted that it clearly charmed Ty, who looked spellbound. Then she caught Seth peeking at Lucy and saw Lucy's answering smile. When she glanced at Cooper, her heart stumbled in her chest.

They were undoubtedly the luckiest six people in the world…the luckiest nine people if you counted the three babies that had brought them together. The luckiest twenty-five people if you counted Madelyn's family into the Bryant clan, and the Bryants definitely counted Madelyn's family as their own. The luckiest five hundred, if you counted the employees of Bryant Development. And fifteen hundred, if you counted the entire small town of Porter.

And Zoe did. Porter was a little place, but it was huge in the way it had been blessed with love and laughter and friends who were family.

That is…they were family if you believed that love meant more than bloodlines.

And Zoe did.

* * * * *

SILHOUETTE *Romance* ®

Matilda Grant signed on to a reality
show to win fifty thousand dollars,
but once she met contestant
David Simpson all the rules changed!

Don't miss a moment of

The Dating Game

by

SHIRLEY JUMP

Silhouette Romance #1795

On sale
December 2005!

Only from Silhouette Books!

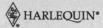

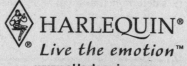

HARLEQUIN®
Presents

Seduction and Passion Guaranteed!

Don't miss our two Christmas-themed stories,
coming in December 2005 only from
Harlequin Presents®!

THE GREEK'S CHRISTMAS BABY
Lucy Monroe
#2506

Greek tycoon Aristide Kouros has a piece of paper to prove
that he's married, but no memory of his beautiful wife, Eden.
Eden loves Aristide, and it's breaking her heart that he has no
recollection of their love. But Eden has a secret that
will bind Aristide to her forever....

CLAIMING HIS
CHRISTMAS BRIDE
Carole Mortimer
#2510

When Gideon Webber meets Molly Barton he wants her badly.
But he is convinced she is another man's mistress.... Three
years on, a chance meeting throws Molly back in his path, and
this time he's determined to claim Molly—as his wife!

www.eHarlequin.com   HPXMAS

COMING NEXT MONTH

#1794 TWELFTH NIGHT PROPOSAL—Karen Rose Smith
Shakespeare in Love
Sometimes tragedy highlights the greatness of love. Of course, Verity Sumpter, who lost her twin, and Leo Montgomery, who lost his wife, wouldn't believe it at first. Yet, as they draw closer, they just might see that the barriers of mistrust that loss erects are best scaled in pairs.

#1795 THE DATING GAME—Shirley Jump
Matilda Grant prefers the Survival TV show she'd applied for originally. At least *there* the chameleons sometimes reveal themselves. On this dating game, she can't tell if she should trust her heart, the bachelors, or—no, probably not—that charmingly ubiquitous David Simpson....

#1796 MEET ME UNDER THE MISTLETOE—
Julianna Morris
Sure, the breezy Shannon O'Rourke coaxed his son's cherished toy rabbit from his grasp—a rare sign of outreach from a child who had just lost his mother. Still, Alex McKenzie is unsettled by her vibrant presence...and the hope she plants in his lonely heart.

#1797 BOUND BY HONOR—Donna Clayton
Men of Honor
Gage Dalton owes Jenna Butler a Life Gift because she saved him during a storm. Yet, even as she makes him marry her, so to better lobby the Tribe for guardianship of her niece, he wonders if perhaps he isn't receiving the more wonderful gift himself....